Prai

The Feminine Art

"Reading *The Feminine Art* has been more than worth my while, it has been a garden of delights! Truly, when I finished it this morning I burst into tears – the ending lives up to all of its promises."

–Frances Kuffel, Author of *Passing For Thin*

"The veils of Chaldean life are lifted as this author takes us through the daily lives of a culture that reaches all the way back to the cross and beyond. Each chapter a book in itself, readers will find themselves walking into the familiar and uncertain, seeing how we each are truly connected to the web of life."

–Charles Gray Wolf, Ph.D.

"Weam Namou is the first novelist in America to touch the heart of the Chaldean community. We highly encourage this feminine experience and consider it to be the first positive seed in our modern culture, with the hope that there's much more to come."

–Salam Romaya, Editor-in-Chief, *The Harp Magazine*

Hermiz Publishing

ISBN 0-9752956-1-6 (hardcover)
ISBN 0-9752956-0-8 (paperback)

Library of Congress Cataloging-in-Publication Data: 2004103692

10 9 8 7 6 5 4 3 2 1

First Edition

Published in the United States of America by:
Hermiz Publishing, Inc.
P.O. Box 4672
Troy, MI 48099   USA
www.HermizPublishing.com
Email: info@HermizPublishing.com

ACKNOWLEDGEMENTS

My utmost gratitude to God, whose Grace throughout this process has been my sufficiency.

Many thanks to Linda Sweeney, who helped plant this novel. To Barnes & Noble's Rochester Writers' Group for wanting it to grow. To Caribou Coffee for providing a hospitable atmosphere for it to blossom. To Frances Kuffel, for catching it with her insight, watering it with her faith and passion, and through her generosity, sharing with others its fruits.

Much love and gratitude to my father's belief in freedom and independence, his love for books, and the Arabic and English languages. To my mother's self-knowledge, her sustained love, and unfailing discipline. To my brothers: George, may God rest his soul; Basim, for having safely brought the family to America; Haithem and Humam, for taking on the father-figure role by providing and protecting, thus allowing me to concentrate on my writing; Adnan, for patiently addressing all my computer illiteracy needs. To my sisters; Basima, may God rest her soul, whose gracefulness I'm happy to now share with the world; Kheelood, for her true Iraqi aura and knowledge of traditional etiquette; Niran, Awatif, Nidhal and Heyam, who have shielded me through rough times and rejoiced with me through good times and wanted the very best for me through all times.

My appreciation goes to all my nineteen nephews, for their humor, sensitivity, and their gallant responses to my requests. To all my precious nieces; Ban, who's our sweetest reminder of her mother, Basima; Sandra, Nora and Dena, whose energetic souls, pure hearts and powerful views on life have been excellent examples for me; Heba, Hadeel, Amorette and Cassandra, whose innocence and virtue remind me why it's important to set examples. A very special thanks to my niece Angela, who from day one, has been assisting and encouraging and counseling and implementing all that her strength could permit into my writing career.

Weam Namou

The Feminine Art

A Hermiz Publishing Book

Chapter 1

Suham awakened long before her husband
and gazed through the bedroom window. Last night's
winds had brought no damage, but a thin sheet of
snow covered Charleston Street as far as the last
orange house on the left, where cars stopped at the
traffic light before heading south of 17 Mile Road.

Suham's route was always south, where, from the
Middle Eastern bakery, La-Shish restaurant and St.
Joseph Chaldean Church, she came closest to smelling the streets of Baghdad. As the lights turned red to
green, she stared at the orange house and wondered
what its lady cooked for supper at night.

When she first came to this country, she'd
thought that Americans only served their families in-
dividual china plates with one piece of steak, a baked
potato, a few spoons of corn or green beans, a glass
of milk and a biscuit. Everyone ate with forks and
knives and napkins. Very neat – eating like kings and
queens and talking about politics instead of shouting
at children with chocolate smeared fingertips, who
touched a clean wall or a new couch.

She'd known people from the Middle East, on the
other hand, to have much too much passion to pay
attention to utensils during eating, so they'd made it

simple – hands and spoons.   Also people from that region were too proud about food to be given one plate of it. More was always better.

There might be an exception to the Lebanese – they were as European as Arabs got because they were as influenced by the French as a daughter was by her mother. Americans weren't really European, though, even if they did use forks and knives. She had never seen Europe, but some friends had told her all about it.

Suham sighed, heavily, while still gazing through the bedroom window. She didn't like snow. So often she tried to befriend it by seeing it through the eyes of children building snowmen, but she couldn't. An entire part of the earth turning white and cold for half a dozen months couldn't appeal to a lady accustomed to sitting on the patio and fanning herself until bedtime. Besides, it was difficult to smell Baghdad in the midst of snow; that city knew only rain, sand blizzards and shish kebab.

One would suspect that living twenty years in Michigan would make her forget Baghdad's heat, but if she forgot that, the next day she would forget her mother's oven baked *kiliecha*, a dessert made for Easter and Christmas, and in a few years, she would have surrendered her identity.

Suham put on her robe and slippers and went to the kitchen to make Turkish coffee and smoke a cigarette. She warmed her cold hands over the stove's heat and waited for the water to boil. She added coffee and sugar to the water and stirred until they smoothly blended together, the same way her personality blended with her husband's, George.

George looked like her perfect match but he really wasn't. He came from an honorable Chaldean – Neo-Babylonian – family who had left their homeland of

Telkaif, a Christian village in the Northern part of
Iraq, long before his parents were born. They were
one of the first to come to Baghdad and live amongst
Muslims and the first to have come to the United
States and live amongst Americans. Such things gave
them superiority, because they told new immigrants
what should and should not be done.

Suham poured the coffee into a cup and went
to the family room. She lit a cigarette and smoked
it while sitting near the window, by the sun. The
winter had stripped the trees naked of their leaves.
Her mother once said nature couldn't handle modern
life and one day, it would surely die – especially in
Michigan, where temperatures could go from sixty
degrees one week, forcing trees into blossom, down to
ten degrees the next week so that the trees froze.

Suham at first couldn't understand the tragedy
of this and her mother must have seen the airhead
expression on her face because she'd explained,
"Imagine a woman going through four miscarriages in
one year."

George came down a few hours later and stood
in front of Suham while fixing the blue collar around
his neck. His square jaw, thick straight eyebrows and
skinny, reluctant-to-smile lips made him look like the
most mature person on earth. He could easily pass
for an ambassador who met with foreign ministers,
not a storeowner who checked the Frito Lay's order
his salesman delivered every Wednesday.

Nothing about George was extraordinarily beauti-
ful, but any woman would die to have his metabolism.
He drank Scotch at any function, constantly ate deep
fried potato chops, and, at work, he spread Hagaan
Daz vanilla ice cream over his Dove chocolate bars.
Yet he was thin, which was highly unusual for a Chal-

dean man married to a good homemaker.

"Can I turn on the light?" he asked most seriously.

She wished he could just turn on the light without making a conversation out of it. But he had lived in America for nearly three decades, since the age of ten, and he'd been told by television that one must communicate in order to be perfect. She didn't mind their talks as much when they spoke Aramaic, the language of ancient Babylon, which was spoken by Jesus Christ and which kept her connected to her deceased mother. This morning started in English. Throughout the day, it would oscillate between English, Arabic and Aramaic.

She said he could go ahead and turn the lights on.

"I didn't make breakfast, sorry," she said.

"That's fine." He came and sat beside her, slipping his hands beneath her nightgown and stroking her leg. His palm felt like a heating pad but his fingertips like a cat's whiskers. She hated cats because they never smiled. They always had their nose up in the air, like the Chaldean women at Sunday Mass who showed off their fur coats, their bleached hair and new spiral perms.

"Yesterday, they said to expect three to four inches of snow," George said, looking outside.

"A weatherman must be the only job where someone can repeatedly screw up without getting fired."

He smiled. "Yeah."

His eyes returned to her body, but before he got too comfortable again, she ruined the mood by asking a simple question – George never grew out of that lovey dovey stage. Suham never got into it.

"Could you have dinner at your mother's tonight?"

He stopped stroking her leg and frowned. How easily she destroyed his happiness, she thought. Other women envied the way George loved her and often saw her as an unappreciative wife. They didn't understand his love was more of a responsibility than it was a comfort. It seemed she was always hearing how terrifically George treated her and sometimes she had to wonder what made her so dense.

Before George fainted from hurt feelings, Suham explained that she'd invited her nephew Michael for dinner and she wanted to have a serious talk with him alone.

"Is it necessary that I'm not here?" George asked.

"Michael doesn't want to have a serious talk and you'd be the perfect distraction." She felt as though she was talking about an eight year old. Michael had recently turned thirty-two.

His head low, George didn't say a word.

That was the responsibility; proving to him she did care for him when half the time she wanted to be left alone. If only he'd stop trying to please her so much, he could improve the things that irritated her about him.

"Well?"

"Well, I'm not going to stay where I'm not wanted."

"It's not like that," she said. "You don't want me in the store. That doesn't make me feel unwanted."

"I don't mind you being in the store."

"You do."

He stared ahead at the wall and she smoked her cigarette. She knew he wanted to elaborate, express how lonely and neglected he felt, but he feared it would upset her. And it would. He centered his happiness around her, even more now that their two children had moved out of the house.

"My mom might've not cooked anything today," he said.

"She has. She told me yesterday she was making lima beans for dinner."

"If you knew yesterday that I wasn't going to have dinner at home, why didn't you say something about it yesterday?"

"Michael hadn't given me a definite answer until after you were sound asleep," she said in the most relaxed manner, keeping in mind how very very much he loved her. "Luckily, your mother wasn't asleep."

He remained quiet. This was quite customary, so she handled it like a professional. "Please, George."

"Alright, fine." Though he sounded irritated. He stood and walked towards the closet.

"Don't come home too late, though. We'll have tea and dessert together."

He put on his jacket and grabbed his keys from the kitchen counter, avoiding eye contact with her.

"And bring some sweets from the bakery. Michael will probably eat what's left of last night's cream caramel."

He looked at her in an angry way, but she knew it was temporary. "I might as well have dessert at my mother's then..."

"I won't have any cream caramel. I'll wait for you."

He nodded but didn't seem convinced she'd do what she promised. She understood. She'd broken her promise once or twice before, and as though he was the media and she a politician, he never let her forget it.

"You're due for a haircut," she said before he touched the doorknob.

He ran his fingers through his thick dark hair

and she smiled slightly.

"Please don't tell me I look like a porcupine."

"I won't." Her smile widened. What gave him such a silly idea? He probably didn't see himself as skinny as the okra she planned on cooking tomorrow.

Suham worried over skinny people's emotional states. Their bodies seemed too fragile to handle thousands of feelings at once, because they had no curves or hills to bypass, so their misery went straight to the bones.

Suham wasn't considered fat, but seven pounds taken off the buttocks and thighs could simplify shopping for pants, not that she wore them much. Aside from grocery stores, she rarely went anywhere without dressing up. The last thing she wanted people who sided with George to say was "Look, and she's not even worth his love."

Chapter 2

When George left the house, Suham went upstairs and changed into stretch pants and a T-shirt. The house wasn't messy – her house never was – but she still vacuumed the family room and mopped the kitchen floor. Since her daughter Nisreen got married and her son Fadi lived in a dorm in Ann Arbor, cleaning had become an addiction. But it wasn't a bad addiction – it kept away terrible thoughts and it firmed up her behind.

The refrigerator had enough leftovers, fruits and vegetables to feed Michael for at least 200 hours, yet she went to Vino's produce market to buy fresh romaine lettuce and beets anyway, as if the roast and potatoes she planned to cook would have been insulted if their company had been a day old. Initially Suham wanted to make Cornish hens tonight, but because Michael's mother cooked Cornish hens as often as she cleaned her dentures, Suham figured Michael was sick of them. Never mind that he claimed them as his favorite dish on earth.

Suham drove to Farmer Jack to buy a roast, but at the checkout counter, she doubted herself. What if Michael didn't enjoy this ton of beef because he'd heard on the news that cows weren't feeling too well lately? And what if the sight of a grilled bird on his dish could open his appetite as widely as the guards could open a castle's door before the queen entered through it?

A can of kernel corn in her left hand and a box of baking soda in her right, both products having been on sale, Suham suddenly paused in the middle of the #3 checkout counter and did an unusual thing. Between the shoppers and shopping cart, the candy and magazine racks, she prayed for Michael's well being.

Michael was not ill, but he worked less often than she made turnip stew, George's least favorite dish. The store his father had left him was run by his uncle, his father's brother. As if he was the Coca Cola salesman and not the owner, he checked in on the store on a weekly basis.

Aside from treating his deceased father's store like a pastime, Michael also resisted following the Chaldean tradition of growing up, getting married and having a family. He didn't realize this tradition was universal. And if he, God forbid, found out this truth, he would nurture his resistance like a child would a lost cat. He absolutely loved rebelling.

Wanting nothing to do with Michael's disappointment, Suham drove her cart back to the meat department and exchanged the roast beef for six Cornish hens. She returned to the checkout counter and prepared her coupons for the 2-liter pop and the bag of sugar.

Suham drove home listening to 690 AM, a Middle Eastern radio station. Arabic songs had words about love that made the body warm and the eyes wet. It hurt being far away from Baghdad, where as a young girl, she sat on soft grass in her father's back yard and listened to Um-Kelthoum while the sun gently stroked her hair.

She remembered one day in particular when she'd loved her back yard more than any other time. She had been petting a white sheep, which had a mark on his belly, the size and color of a red apple. Her mother stood on the patio, yelling at her father for "again" having brought home an unwanted sheep. They were hard to kill, she'd complained, hard to clean, hard to cook.

Her father tried to explain his feelings, but by then, her mother had disappeared back into the house. She returned five minutes later with the next-door neighbor's boy, Ahmad.

Suham giggled at the sight of Ahmad, a giant in size, but a turtle at heart. Her father and Ahmad pulled up their sleeves and marched towards her, their heads slightly bent, like bulls without horns.

"What are you guys doing?" Suham said before they touched the animal.

They looked confused and she took full advantage of that. "If you intended to slaughter it from the very beginning, you shouldn't have let it sit here with me so I can get attached to it."

She began to defend the life of the sheep as though it was her own brother. Why not, she thought? He had the same hazel eyes as her brother and he may be even nicer. Besides, what she was doing was fun.

While she declared all sorts of things, her father cleared his throat a dozen times. But it didn't help him speak any better. Suham then purposely kept quiet, making him even more uncomfortable. Her mother must have noticed the strange delay because she stormed towards them, like an over-weight bull-fighter.

Suham wished she had kept her big mouth shut. She always wanted to flaunt her intelligence, never thinking her own words would have her attached to the sheep. Unfortunately, she couldn't rewind the scene, be a good girl and allow her father to do his job.

Her mother stood over Suham, furious, both fists on her hips. The battle ended instantly, of course, and the sheep became a five-day feast. Her mother had cut its skin into squares, so for a more special occasion, she'd make *pacha*, stuffed sheep's skin sealed lightly with a needle and black thread – black so everyone could see it and wouldn't choke on it. Then she sliced the meat into large chunks and placed half of them in the freezer. She made *tashreeb*, a special broth of chickpeas, onions and strong spices, with the rest of the meat.

Suham promised herself she wouldn't eat the meat out of respect for the hazel eyes, but when it was served, her heart hardened. She craved the large tender chunks of meat that floated in the bowl of thick broth, like a shiny frog in a pond. She wanted, like her siblings, to drink the broth from the bowl and make a hearty sandwich of meat, raw green onions, tomatoes and radishes.

She hadn't really believed she could save the sheep forever, anyhow. She'd only thought it courageous to have tried.

Suham parked her car in the driveway. As she grabbed the grocery bags out of the trunk, she saw Mrs. Wozniak, her next-door neighbor, get her mail. Avoiding Mrs. Wozniak was as unlikely as seeing the sun and the stars in the sky at the same time. She wasn't the average American who worked 9 to 5 and minded her own business. She took her neighborhood too seriously, as if it was an engineering project.

"Suham," Mrs. Wozniak called.

Suham lifted her head, smiled and waved.

"Careful, it's slippery."

"I know. How are you, Lisa?" She prayed the answer would be short, because she hated the whole world when snow visited it.

"Oh, worn out and beat." She laughed like no other woman who truly felt worn out and beat would laugh.

"God help you."

Suham slipped a little as she walked but she quickly gained her balance. Had she fallen, Mrs. Wozniak would never forgive herself, the Cornish hens would scatter, making her front yard a winter farm, and the dinner with Michael, which her sister Wadi, Michael's mother, had been counting on for days, would have to be canceled – or to be more accurate, postponed.

"Careful, Suham!"

Suham forced out a smile.

"Boy, it's terrible out here – now go on inside before you get yourself in trouble." And for no apparent reason, the woman giggled.

Suham rushed inside with a sigh of relief. She wished she could be friendlier to Lisa, but she feared any kindness would only force her into unwanted intimacies with her.

As Suham put the groceries away it began to snow again. She felt terribly cold and tired and wanted to rest a half hour before she started cooking. But the moment she thought she had a chance to relax, her sister Wadi called.

Wadi's husband had died years ago, and like most Chaldean women her age, she spoke little English and didn't work. She therefore had enough energy to talk to relatives on the phone from the time she put in her dentures in the morning until she took them out at night. Aside from Wadi, Suham had three older brothers. They rarely called, because that was their wives' job.

Wadi and Suham talked for twenty minutes – a reasonable amount of time, Suham thought. As much as she loved her sister, she had better things to do with the rest of her day, although she wasn't really sure what those things might be.

But for Wadi, twenty minutes wasn't enough, because after the first conversation, she continued to phone; once as Suham was slicing the dinner potatoes into halves, again while she was browning the almonds and raisins on a skillet for the rice, and a third time as she chopped the romaine lettuce for salad.

Suham nearly went mad. How can a person be so addicted to the phone that they use it as often as a writer uses a pen? She didn't protest, however, because she knew that protesting meant another two hours on the phone. Wadi would defend whatever accusations were made against her or she'd ask to clarify any complaints. At the end, Wadi would come out pleased, while Suham would need three aspirins. So Suham patiently listened as she prepared the salad for Michael, knowing the chance to rest before Michael came was ruined.

Wadi talked about her hemorrhoid and arthritis problems, how the doctors were not helpful because they had no medications to ease her pain, and how Michael didn't treat her as good as other Chaldean boys treated their mothers. He either came home at three o'clock in the morning or he didn't come home at all, leaving her alone in a two-story house. If she was dying from a heart attack, no one could save her. If a thief broke into their home, no one would kill him. She felt more abandoned by her son than she did by her deceased husband, who in spirit, she claimed, still resided in her house.

She asked Suham to make Michael see the harm he was causing. Her blood pressure had risen, her sugar too, and for the past two weeks, diarrhea.

"You keep repeating `say this, say that'." Suham restrained herself no more. "I'm not stupid. I know what to say."

If she sounded aggravated it was because she'd poured the olive oil into the salad when she should've waited until Michael came. Now she'd have to start chopping new lettuce and tomatoes, or else she'd have to serve Michael a soggy salad, which she was incapable of doing.

Maybe an answering machine could make her life easier. But no Chaldean home she knew of had one. It would take forever to teach elders how to use it. Children, by playing with it, might break it. And having a machine tell a sister or friend that no one could get to the phone right now so please leave a name, number and a brief message was cold – and even rude. People could call a doctor's office for that.

"Tell him he forgot to get my medicine too, will you?"

"As if he'll do it, anyway," Suham said harshly, even though she knew she'd hurt her sister's feelings. "He'll forget again. For God's sake, Wadi, don't you know him by now?"

"I think I sometimes do, but I guess I really don't." Her voice saddened and Suham knew she wanted sympathy.

"Even after I tell you time and time again?"

"You don't tell me anything!" Wadi's voice sprung high, the way a mosquito does before it gets squashed. "You cover for Michael and he covers for you."

"And what have I got to cover, aside from my

breasts and my behind?"

Wadi grunted and mumbled something here and there and Suham avoided it.

"Tell me the truth." Wadi's tone completely changed, which signaled that a new topic would be presented. "Did Georgette's daughter-in-law really steal her black pepper container just to pinch her nerves?"

"Who told you that?" Suham was interested to know, Georgette being her sister-in-law's mother-in-law, but not the daughter-in-law just spoken of.

As Wadi informed her of who said what to whom and when and how, Suham placed the salad bowl in the refrigerator and she soaked the rice in water. And when the story became more interesting still, Georgette's daughter-in-law having thrown her husband's clothes into the basement and then having locked herself in her own room, Suham figured it wasn't so bad after all, preparing dinner while talking on the phone.

She scrambled a few eggs in a bowl, brushed them over the potatoes, seasoned the Cornish hens with salt and garlic powder and placed everything in the oven.

Then she came up for air.

"Listen Wadi, I'll call you after Michael leaves," she said. "Otherwise, the rice might turn into custard."

She tried to lie down but another lobster's claw, her sister-in-law Alia, grabbed her beforehand. They'd barely greeted each other before Alia attacked Suham for not having asked about her for two weeks, during which Alia had had a severe cold.

Suham apologized, made a dozen excuses for not having called and then gave Alia Arabic blessings. Meanwhile, she cooked the rice.

When she finally finished with Alia, she stretched her neck, turned off all appliances and smoked a cigarette while sitting by the window. There her mind traveled overseas to Al-Mansoor's exotic *souks* and replayed the days when she was considered a girl. Suham had enjoyed that title, which females from the Middle East lost once they married or became old maids. Only then were they considered women.

Having married at sixteen, Suham felt her girl-hood was cut short. She wished she'd remained single longer, to achieve ladyship status and continue being admired by men with moustaches while walking down the streets of Al-Mansoor, especially on Fridays – that day being to Muslims what Sundays were to Westerners.

During those days, when no pretty girl allowed her beauty to be unnoticed, Wadi walked beside Su-ham, behaving like a brother. Wadi had found those handsome men with big arms and devilish eyes disgusting, but Suham was mesmerized by their interest. Wadi tried hiding Suham's curves and pretty face by marching in front of her, her ruthless frown a weapon. Thank heavens, though, nothing had stopped those men from behaving like the average Arabic man and treasuring, even weakening to, female beauty. But eventually, like they were rabbits eating her lettuce, Wadi shooed them away with grunts.

Suham finished her cigarette and put it in the ashtray. She dreamt of being in the *souk*, surrounded by merchants and yards of fabric – silk, velvet and cotton, from the color of bright yellow to that of orange red – as she fell asleep on the couch. She didn't wake up until Michael arrived for dinner at eight o'clock, an hour late.

Chapter 3

ichael checked inside the oven, tasted a small piece of a Cornish hen and told his aunt they were delicious. Then he lifted the pot's lid and was about to eat from it when Suham shrieked, "Don't do that! It's bad luck!"

"Mom lets me eat from it." He dipped his hand in the pot and took a raisin, while she shook her head.

"That's why she has so many problems with you," she said. "She lets you do whatever your heart desires and unfortunately your heart desires sin."

"Nothing wrong with that." Michael knew a little Aramaic and was fluent in Arabic and English. But he mostly used English to deliver his strong points across.

He went to wash his hands in the bathroom while Suham set up the table as delicately as a doctor would stitch a wound. Next to his dish of three Cornish hens and rice sat a bowl of pickled cabbage and cauliflower, a plate of green onions, beets and parsley, a glass of pop, a bowl of salad and a basket of pita bread. She hoped the table would impress him as much as it did her.

Michael came back, drying his hands with a towel for two minutes straight. He must be the cleanest

man on earth, she thought, because he was as petri-
fied of germs as girls were of spiders. Yet he loved sin,
which could do more harm to his health than dirt. He
and George should have beers together one week and
exchange habits. George could learn to become less
cold and Michael less bad.

Michael sat at the table and immediately started
eating. Suham paid close attention to how he anxiously tore a hen apart and repeatedly stuffed his
mouth with rice, so she made sure he had two serv-
ings, and after he finished his third hen, she insisted
he eat one more.

"I can't," he said. "I'll kill myself."

"Okay, half."

He agreed and she didn't dare insist again. Michael would rather starve than overeat. Overeating
was the unhealthiest thing on earth. Of course,
drinking liquor and partying all night were not.

Michael dropped his spoon over his empty plate,
sat back and stared ahead with a dazed expression,
which represented his need for tea, as clearly as the
donation basket in church represented a priest's need
of dollars.

Suham served him a cup of tea with a small slice
of cream caramel and watched him eat the dessert
while she smoked another cigarette. She admired her
nephew, probably no more than any other Chaldean
aunt who was close to her sister did. Everyone knew,
if that everyone was Chaldean, that a sibling's child
was spoiled more than one's own, because along with
loving them well, there wasn't the pressure of raising
them well.

Suham had four other nephews, her brothers'
children, but they were barely teenagers. She had
nieces as well – eight of them – but like most Chaldean
children, including her very own, they were closer to

their mothers' side of the family, even though in the Middle Eastern tradition, the aunts and uncles from the father's side held more honor and prestige.

Wadi, Suham's only sister and the oldest of the siblings, had one child, whom she named after his grandfather, Mikhael, and three miscarriages. These circumstances led her to accept her fate of infertility much more quickly than Suham would have if she had been in the same situation.

Friends and family tried to console Wadi for not having ten little ones – it was a time when people, in regards to babies, believed in the multiplication table – by saying, "It's God's Will." Such words might have comforted Wadi, but they did nothing for Suham. She would have felt proud, and safer for her sister's sake, with more family relations. And these same people also said, "At least God gave you a boy", which Suham agreed with perfectly.

But Michael and Suham's relationship went beyond nephew and aunt. They were connected by blood but were only five years apart in age; they became friends before they understood the title each of them held above or beneath the other. Had she not been married, Suham would have forgotten their birth labels altogether, which Michael had already taken the liberty of doing.

"This cream caramel is soggy," he complained.

"I made it last night, that's why."

He went back to finishing the dessert.

When she was sure he didn't have anything left to say, she revealed her intentions. "Your mother and I want to find you a wife."

He raised his eyes from the spoon to hers, giving her an uncomfortable stare, like he knew this dinner was a peanut and he the elephant. He intimidated Suham only briefly, and she hurried her lecturing before he could protest further.

"Honestly, Michael, what else is left in life besides a young beautiful wife to love and bear your children?"

He grinned. "A beautiful madam."

She rolled her eyes and exasperated. "What on earth would you do with her that you haven't done already?"

"I'd tell her I love her and wouldn't feel guilty for it."

She smoked her cigarette, watched his playful stare and wondered how she could resist his charm without smiling. She remembered her sister Wadi's wounded heart, which was what Wadi claimed time and time again anyway – whether it was true or not Suham couldn't swear – and that helped her remain serious.

"I'm not ready yet," he declared, his mouth filled with a gulp of tea. "I don't understand why it bothers any of you that I'm single."

"Because at your age, it's not natural."

"Says who?"

"Says God."

"Adam didn't meet Eve until he was a 1000 years old."

"Years were measured differently then."

"Even if they were, they'd be what – 500 years?"

"Even fewer."

"I don't think so," he said. "People lived longer before – it's a fact."

"You're talking about the Old Testament and the Old Testament is part fiction!" Her face was getting hot. It was times like this when she wished she had taken on the true role of an aunt and pampered him with only food and compliments, not admiration. Sometimes she believed she was no better than his mother.

"The Bible is educational and simple, because see – back then, when people wanted to do it, they did it."

She was confused. "Do what?"

"It!"

"Ah," she sighed, leaning back. "And `it' is so educational?"

"Listen to me, there are two things that make the world go round – money and sex." His eyes eased up and he shrugged his shoulders. "Of course, money meant nothing then because Christopher Columbus hadn't found America yet."

She couldn't help from smiling. She considered whether she ought to give up on him for the night since once again he refused to be cornered into a serious discussion. But to have more patience and to put a little more effort into cornering him would be easier than to kick her husband out of the house again and prepare another feast, not to mention Wadi's reaction. She'd be outraged to hear that the task, which she'd swear should be as simple for Suham as peeling garlic, wasn't accomplished.

Michael must have mistaken her silence as a sign of encouragement because he continued earnestly. "If today, like in the olden days, doing it would be looked at as harmless – as natural – as asking a girl out for a cup of cappuccino, there wouldn't be any wars."

"How pretty life must be for a man who thinks this way." She wished she were in his shoes, acting immature and getting away with it.

His finger wiped the sugar syrup off the plate and he licked it. She smoked, staring at him silently, as she prepared what she'd say next. If she pressured him, he would get mad and rebel. If she didn't talk, she'd soon find herself running out of time. At eleven o'clock George locked up the store, and at twenty past eleven, he came home. Which meant she had exactly seventeen minutes left.

"Michael, sweetheart, the point is..."

"The point is God made Adam and Eve, not husband and wife," he interrupted. "I have many Eves. You should be happy for me, damn it."

"Oh, really? Then why aren't you happy with them?"

"Because you guys think I'm miserable."

"You think if we knew you were truly happy, which you truly are not, we wouldn't see it in you and thank God for it?"

"No, actually you wouldn't, because you think being happy is sleeping with my wife in a king size bed. Maybe happiness to me is something else. Maybe to me, being happy is screwing a girl off the street in a back alley of a Detroit neighborhood."

She shook her head disapprovingly and in her heart she cussed at Wadi for having spoiled this man to the degree that he thought it quite normal to act quite vulgar. He might have been an only child, and a boy to top it off, but he wasn't a prince or a saint – although yes he might have been more charming than both.

"That's coarse," she said, like a proper aunt should. "We might be around the same age, but I'm your aunt."

"So what?"

"Michael!"

"Look, you got married too young, I'll get married too old. That's fair."

"Back then, I wasn't considered too young."

"Fifteen!"

"Sixteen!"

"I thought it was too young, but did you hear me

complain?"

"For God's sakes Michael," she said, sternly. "You try to convince yourself what you want is liquor and whores, not because it's true but because you don't know if you're qualified enough for something better."

He lowered his head and didn't say a word. Before saying meaner things that could hurt him deeply – she was capable of doing that to people when she felt frustrated – she took a minute to calm herself; she lifted the empty dessert plate and spoon in front of him and placed them in the sink.

"Do you want more tea?" she asked, her voice still not as friendly as when they'd first started this discussion.

"Why?" he said, softly.

"Because count on this being a long evening."

"Great! Then do you have Scotch?"

Her roughness immediately eased up as she closed her eyes and smiled. "It's difficult enough talking to you while you're sober."

"You guys don't have Scotch here anyway," he mumbled, "because you guys are a bunch of sissies."

She poured more tea for him. As she stared into the cup, where she saw her eyes and lashes looking back up at her, she felt the way she did in church. She always blocked out the priest's sermon when it dealt with his need of money, and she was simply mesmerized by the candle light near the altar. Feeling now what she felt in that moment in church, she prayed that Michael would find himself a girl to love and adore him.

They spent the rest of the night in the family room, where Michael turned on the television and watched the Red Wings play against the St. Louis Blues. He tried to tell Suham how the Red Wings were the best team, even when they lost. Their problem was that they always screwed up in the play-offs. They made more money from tickets and T-shirts and jerseys than any other team in sports. Hockey was the best. If only it got international coverage, it'd be the biggest sport on earth.

Suham listened with all her might, because it wasn't easy to grasp information about sports. In Baghdad, there was only soccer. In America, there were half a dozen sports and fifty professional teams and NBA's and NCAA's, penalties and fouls stacked on top of fouls, like the soup cans stacked over each other in George's store, aisle number four.

"Their uniforms are the nicest ones I've ever seen any team wear," Suham said. She was honestly impressed with the red and white colors.

"Yeah, it's the best!" He watched the game with great interest, as if he wanted to eat the television set and have a Red Wing skate inside his stomach.

She allowed a few minutes of silence between them – so he could digest the game and be satisfied, before she forced the issue of marriage back into the picture. She asked him if he had a girlfriend, and he said several – but none of them she'd approve of, or respect for that matter.

"Why not?" she asked.

"Well, they're whores."

"Can we find someone for you then – your mother and I?"

"Go ahead," he said, obviously trying to concentrate on the game. "I won't stop you. Just make sure she has big tits."

"Michael, for God's sakes...

"Hey, don't I have any word in this?"

"You have. Anyway, you know my taste is good. I'll find you the most beautiful, sweetest girl you've seen."

"Fine, but I won't get married right away. I want to have more fun."

"You can have fun with your wife."

"Yes, but if she's a virgin and she doesn't know how to do it, then..."

"Then you'll teach her," she suggested.

He smiled a naughty smile. "Can you imagine what a bitch it would be if I come to teach her and she taught me instead?"

What a stupid boy, she thought. He didn't know the opposite sex, despite his many adventures with them. Unless she was an amazon or he himself was a little boy, it wasn't in women's nature to teach men perversion of a higher level than that which was already in a man's head. If women did use their hips and thighs seductively to love a man, it was because they were exotic, not perverted; or they were in love, or because they had to. Many men could not open their hearts unless they undid their pants first.

Michael jumped from the couch and hollered. Someone scored she figured, and from his disappointment, it must be the St. Louis Blues.

"Michael, please," she begged, seeing he wouldn't sit back down.

His eyes still on the television screen, he slammed the table with his fist. She called his name several times, and when that didn't work, she demanded that he pay attention to her and not the game. He finally agreed.

"Listen, you needn't worry about ending up with the wrong girl," she said. "Wadi and I will ask around about her."

"How the hell are you going to know if a girl hasn't had a pimp?" His eyes were bewildered, as if his comment held any weight. "Trust me, this is as risky a business as dealing drugs."

She loved him, absolutely adored his charm, but she wished he'd ease up on his vulgarity, because every time he swore or drew her a picture worse than whole body tattoos, she lost focus on what she was trying to say.

"That's what's wrong with American television," she said, thinking of her childhood in Baghdad, where television programs were available only eight hours a day and offered on only two channels. Fridays they ran longer, from ten in the morning until midnight. "They make a man hallucinate that such things exist."

"Television? I don't watch soap operas, only sports."

"It has nothing to do with watching it. It has to do with believing in it."

"Oh, Jesus."

"Back home, they showed genuine love stories on TV."

"I remember back home."

"You remember it but you don't appreciate its value."

"Not everything there had value."

"We're talking about family life," she said, tightly. "Not the government."

"Oh, what the hell! I said okay, find me a wife. I want a wife, I do."

She sat back and smiled. "Listen, I won't bring this subject up again – ever."

"Yes, you will."

"I won't. I promise."

"You will."

"Okay, I will, but not tonight." She put out her cigarette in the ashtray and walked to one of the kitchen cupboards. "Listen, George's cellular phone is dead. Will you take a look at it for me?"

"Is it the batteries?"

She handed him the phone. "Hmm, no. I don't think it's that simple."

"Nothing's that simple – isn't that a bitch?"

She stood still, her hands on her hips. "If someone heard you talking, they'd think you have all the responsibilities of the world. They'd never guess you're catered to when the sun goes up and when it comes back down."

Michael laughed. "I'll have to take this phone with me and fix it at home. I can't leave until the game is over, though."

"Alright, *habbibi*, but do me a favor. Be a little kinder to your mother."

"Why, has she complained about me lately?"

She arched her brows. "Oh no, not at all."

Michael continued to watch the game in the family room. She on the other hand made herself a cup of Turkish coffee and had another cigarette while sitting by the window in the living room.

She saw Lisa's husband park his car in the driveway. He was a chemist, so he didn't have to deal with shoplifters and Budweiser salesmen, like George. Lisa must be slicing the roast right now and tossing the salad. Then she would make Maxwell House coffee and serve her husband a slice of the chocolate-layered cake she'd bought from Big Boy's restaurant two miles down. She would wear her sweat pants afterwards and lay next to him on the couch. They'd watch the news and kiss each other's hands, like in the nightly sitcoms or the movies.

George would love that lifestyle, but she didn't have the time to live it. Instead she was a brilliant brain chef for friends and family, taking a problem and blending it with syrupy words there, spicing it up with ancient wisdom here, and voila, a delicious solution was baked – out of a recipe that could never be described on paper. When it came to George, however, she used real food, like *kubba* or the yogurt, garlic and cucumber salad, to resolve problems.

Chapter 4

🐫

he fact that Michael agreed on getting married meant less to Wadi than it did to Suham. Wadi wasn't convinced that her son's submission was sincere rather than a scheme to divert his aunt's own scheme. She treated the subject as worryingly as if it was a needle that was lost in the middle of a beige carpet.

Suham wasn't surprised by her sister's reaction. This wasn't the first time Wadi had mistakenly thought she'd been asked to do cartwheels. "I expected this, really," Suham said. "I mean you make a big deal out of cooking *fassoulyah*."

From cannelloni beans, the argument then tilted to eggplant casseroles and cucumber stews for Saturday night. That was the one night of the week, every week, that Suham slept in Wadi's guestroom, the most disoriented room in Wadi's house.

Technically speaking, the room wasn't messy, especially if one didn't put into consideration that the mauve curtains clashed with the blue bed linens and the brass bed with the cherry wooden dresser; or that the countless souvenirs, gifts and statuettes confused the most sensible eye; or that the Jesus Christ, the Virgin Mary and family pictures covered the walls and mirror like carpeting.

On several occasions Suham fought with her sister to improve the room's décor. Wadi always cried "No", but if Suham had really wanted to, she'd turn the house upside down faster than she did a cake that just came out of the oven. She needn't get permission first.

Suham didn't sleep at Wadi's house every Saturday night because she fought with George every Saturday night – although their Chaldean acquaintances might have perceived it that way. Maybe any American would too. She did it simply because she'd needed to take a break often.

Suham didn't explain her behavior to anyone, nor did she bother inventing excuses for it. But out of respect for her husband and family, she was cautious to keep this secret to herself.

In the beginning, Wadi had happily encouraged Suham's visits. It didn't take but three visits, however, for Wadi to frown, and accuse Suham of being cold-hearted, unrealistic, and undeserving.

"For God's sakes, why does it bother you that I'm here?" Suham asked. "I'm keeping you company, aren't I?"

"I didn't expect you to make this a habit."

"But there are good habits and there are bad habits – this isn't bad."

"It doesn't bother me, it worries me," Wadi said in a deep way. "I respect George and I feel guilty about him staying in a big house all alone."

"You're exaggerating. Just like you put too many potatoes and peas in your *biryani* but not enough chicken."

"People die for my *biryani!*"

Suham smiled, knowing she'd touched the most sensitive nerve. She always teased Wadi about her

cooking instead of directly complaining about it.
Wadi's cooking was good, but she tended to cut back
on the ingredients that were difficult to attain in Iraq,
like chicken, eggs or milk, even though these items
were as plenty in America as water.

"Alia will soon find out, you know," Wadi threatened.

That got Suham's attention.   Her youngest
brother's wife Alia kept Chaldean news floating within
the community on a regular basis.   But in order for
the story to be published by her puffy lips and gapped
teeth, it must first be thick and juicy, or else she'd
edit it enough times to make it so, because in the end,
it must fill a woman's curiosity as much as a porter-
house steak filled a man's stomach.

"What you're doing is horrible, Suham!"

Suham smiled at her sister's strength.   It was like
a hot air balloon under the impression it would reach
the clouds despite the power of the tornado who came
to pay it a visit.   "Well, then, do you deny me your
home?"

"Please, don't be cruel."   Wadi's eyes turned
softer, pleading for forgiveness, probably.   Or sympathy.   Suham didn't want to spoil her by giving her
either one.

"I just want to let you know I don't approve."

Suham wondered how her sister had abruptly become the victim in all this.   "You don't have to let me
know anything.   I know you are so good, you hate for
George to think you're taking me away from him.   But
George is good too, and he knows I'm forcing myself
into your home."

At eight-fifteen Sunday morning, after the sisters
quarreled about the sincerity of Michael's intentions
and about the cannelloni beans and eggplants, Suham

heard Wadi shouting from downstairs. She stared at the ceiling for a few seconds, trying to understand the gist of the fight before joining in. It was a given that the shouting had to do with Michael, but she wished to find out what exactly he'd done wrong this time.

She hurried out of bed and head downstairs the second Wadi's voice grew louder and her own curiosity became more intense. Halfway to the living room, she came to a halt at the sight of a blonde girl picking up her purse and dropping it and picking it up again and dropping it again while fumbling towards the door, barefoot and terrified.

The girl wore a shiny green skirt with a brown tank top and dark nylons. Aside from the dry mascara dust circling her eyes and a line of lipstick smeared across her left cheek, aside from her tangled hair, she was a pretty girl. Her blue eyes managed to radiate, despite her messiness.

Wadi was shooing the girl outside with a rag, the way she did with flies in the summer. Michael stood behind Wadi, mute, as if he wasn't part of the problem. The girl finally made it outside, her purse and coat and high-heeled shoes curled into a ball within her arms. A gust of wind entered the house afterwards and Wadi hurried to shut the door. Then like a sergeant, she reprimanded Michael.

"*Ibn al-kalb!*"

Wadi always began by calling Michael a son-of-a-dog.

"You've shamed my house and my name!"

"Jesus Christ!"

"Hush! I don't want God, Jesus, Mary or anyone holy on that filthy tongue of yours. The only thing your mouth deserves is chestnut shells and banana peals."

Suham didn't want to get involved yet, because it

was too early in the morning to spray her intelligence into the air. Besides, there was plenty of that kind of perfume going around already. In less than a minute, however, Wadi's wild eyes spotted her.

"Did you see her?"

Suham looked to the ground. She couldn't begin to speak because in these kinds of situations, Wadi, as Michael's mother, had to first yell more, swear more, or lecture more. It was a custom in all Arabic homes. Kind of.

"If you knock on every Chaldean door," Wadi said to Michael, "and ask them about me – Wadi, Naeim Toma's oldest daughter – they'd say she's respectful, she's honest, she almost became a nun once. Now they'll say she raised a bastard!"

"Good, then we won't have to keep it a secret anymore."

Wadi's head snapped towards Suham, reminding her of a pigeon. Suham had to stop herself from smiling and spoiling her sister's dramatic scene.

"Evil eyes – they started the day he was born."

Michael gasped in disbelief, a gesture he often made when his mother mentioned superstitions. Anytime a misfortune knocked on Wadi's door, especially when it concerned Michael, she accused the entire Chaldean community of it. As though every Chaldean in Michigan did nothing with their time but put voodoo on her son.

Wadi's facial expression turned calm and serene. "Today we'll buy a bottle of Scotch and a box of candy – nothing too fancy. And find me a picture of you, Michael, with half your body showing, from head to waist."

"I don't have one."

"You have hundreds."

"Not by myself."

"Don't be ridiculous, you must have at least one."

"I have a couple. But they're of me naked."

"Find me a decent picture, or *rah akutlak.*"

Wadi threatened to kill Michael on a regular basis, even though never once did she slap him. "We'll take it with the liquor and chocolate to Father Jalal and we'll have him scare off evil spirits."

"I know how to scare off evil spirits myself," Michael said. "No need to pay that crook a bottle of Scotch and candy to have him jack off on my picture while getting drunk and fat."

"Michael!" both women screeched.

"You should be ashamed," Wadi scorned. "Father Jalal is a good man."

"He built a house big enough for the entire city of Detroit – all from our money, all for himself. Charity, charity, he cries every damn sermon."

"How do you know? You never attend church. Besides, he's a priest. He deserves a house."

"A house, not a mansion."

Her eyes opened as wide as a cucumber ring. "It's okay to spend thousands of dollars on bitches when they give you a headache and me an ulcer. It's too much, thought, to give a dime to the church. At least God has blessed our family for generations."

He shook his head.

"But I tell you, if our walls burst today –"

Suham felt her sister should stop the nagging before everyone got so intoxicated by it that they'd need a designated driver.

"— I have you to thank. Your sins have grown bigger than the sky."

"In that case, it's too late to go to Father Jalal."

Suham had warned Wadi time and time again not to push the issue of church down Michael's throat, because he not only hated it, he manipulated the direction of the conversation by it. A man like Michael needed God Almighty to gently sneak up from behind and whisper common sense to him, not stand in front of him wearing a black robe and holding a microphone.

Wadi finally gave up on the notion of dragging Michael to church and insisted on having Father Jalal to bless her house instead.

"Is she serious?" Michael interrupted, addressing Suham and looking as innocent as an apple. "She thinks I'm a demon who needs to be saved by a crook?"

"Never mind that," Suham said, tired of their childish quarrels. "Do you think what you did was nice?"

"What, blaspheming Father Jalal? It was appropriate, I'd say."

She stared at him hard. He could behave like a wild bird in front of Wadi, but in front of her, she expected him to stand as straight as a soldier, and be as honest as an Armenian.

Michael gave up and became the Armenian soldier. "Look, I didn't commit a crime. I met this girl, she didn't have a ride, I was too drunk to drive her home, and we ended up here."

Suham didn't comment; she just shook her head disapprovingly. She didn't want him to get as irritated by her as he did by his mother.

"I was trying to be a good civilian, damn it."

Suham listened to a little more of his nonsense before a painting on the wall distracted her attention. It was of a large pink bird standing beside a green hat with a yellow ribbon. It was new but must have been bought from a garage sale. The painting was on thick paper, it had no frame, and it was ripped an inch from the top.

Suham frowned, approached the wall and stared at the painting with awe. Tearing this painting would get her closer to throwing out Wadi's other memorabilia. She lightly touched the painting and Wadi screamed, "Suham!"

Suham's hands quickly brought the painting down and tore it in half before Wadi could save it. When Suham looked up, she saw Michael's amused smile and Wadi's indescribable expression. She wondered what had suddenly possessed her.

Wadi looked sadly over the torn painting, the way the Virgin Mary looked over Jesus while he lay in her arms. Suham's strength felt good. Her strength had gotten bored of her, especially since her daughter discovered what a kiss could do and her son what a corvette would cost, and had abandoned her. It had probably taken refuge in another woman's body, until Suham came to her senses.

A tour of Wadi's house would gain her back her strength. She'd start by shaking off the few crystals left in the dinning room's chandelier, then move onto throwing out the forty or so empty pita bread bags tucked between the refrigerator and cupboards.

Suham left Wadi mourning the loss of the painting and dashed into the kitchen. She pulled down the plastic green peppers and squash hanging from a rope from the ceiling. Her eyes sought out other things she'd always hated, but her mind was so hungry it didn't know where to start. She heard Wadi behind her yelling, "*Bas! Bas!*"

Suham didn't think it was enough! enough! though. And she wouldn't have stopped had the house not turned as quiet as a library.

"Michael, that American girl is still here!" Wadi gasped.

Suham felt the entire weight in the house shifting towards the living room window. She followed the weight and, pressing the blinds, saw the blonde girl sitting by the tree, on the snow.

"Shit, I forgot she doesn't have a car!"

"Go, go drive her home, poor thing," Wadi said as sweetly as if talking about a friend. "She must be frozen by now."

Michael grabbed his car keys from the kitchen counter, his jacket from over the couch, he said goodbye and rushed outside. Suham felt much calmer now and wondered where the previous craziness had gone.

Wadi sat on the chair. "Go get a robe before you catch a cold."

"I'm fine."

"That boy doesn't like to see me rest." Wadi stared ahead. She had obviously forgotten about the torn painting, proving how much it had meant to her. "Always falling out of trees and almost drowning and getting hit with bricks and metal pipes – and remember that time when a broken glass bottle nearly scratched his eyeball."

Suham sat down on the couch opposite the chair. She and Wadi looked exhausted, like they'd just finished the hardest task in making *pacha*, which was the stitching of the sheep's skin with a needle and thread after having stuffed it with rice, meat, tomato paste and spices.

The energy Suham had minutes ago vanished. She wished the blond girl hadn't distracted her. Had she gone on and on in that way, perhaps she could have forever stopped tolerating whatever stood in front of her. Whatever that was.

"I wonder if Michael would get along with Bahija's daughter," Wadi said. "What's her name – Ghada, I think?"

"Ghada is two feet tall and a thousand pounds."

Wadi frowned. "Stop it. No one could say a bad thing about Ghada."

"Except that she's fat."

"I don't know what you're talking about. Her skin is as white as *leban*."

Suham shrugged. In Iraq people complimented a girl's face or skin by comparing her either to yogurt, the way Wadi just did, or clotted cream, because both were white, smooth, and delicious. Ghada's skin wasn't smooth or white, and by no means could it be delicious, even to somebody with a stuffed up nose.

Wadi asked Suham to scramble eggs and hot dogs. They walked to the kitchen and Suham lit a cigarette before she started breakfast. The second she saw Suham's smoke, Wadi waved it away with both hands. Suham prayed her sister wouldn't complain.

"Put it out or I'll get nauseous."

Suham rolled her eyes and smoked the cigarette anyway.

"Suham, please, what are you doing to yourself—"

Rolling her eyes again, Suham thought how she'd give anything to be alone this minute, lost in old memories. If Wadi drove to the market for orange juice or parsley, Suham could swallow at least ten cigarettes and relax. But Wadi didn't drive!

Then another idea perhaps. Wadi loved parsley with her eggs and soups and fish; last night she had complained she had run out of it. Maybe Suham could offer to go to the market herself and pig out on cigarettes while driving the car and pushing the shopping cart.

Suham turned to mention the parsley, but she

saw Wadi chatting endlessly about cigarettes and Michael and Bahija's daughter. Suham thought it best to keep quiet. Evidently Wadi wasn't in the mood for parsley. What happened with Michael this morning caused enough excitement to destroy any other cravings she would normally have.

"Put it out, I can't bear it," Suham heard again.

The cigarette tumbled into the sink. The weekends at Wadi's house were beginning to lose their flavor, like over-toasted bread and six-hour-old tea and over-boiled cauliflower. She absolutely must find herself a better bed-and-breakfast retreat.

"On the Arabic station yesterday," Wadi said, "they said that anyone who smelled cigarette smoke died."

Suham cooked the eggs and hot dogs and served them to Wadi on a plate.

"That's what made you so nervous first thing this morning. Tearing up pictures and bringing down walls..."

Poor Wadi didn't realize that had it not been for the cigarettes, she'd broken the television set and the stereo instead of the garage sale items.

Chapter 5

🐎

Like a good party, Sunday morning's events entertained Wadi for hours afterwards. Suham went along with her as she criticized the scene and laughed about it. But at twelve-twenty, Suham decided to leave. "I want to rest before Nisreen's dinner party."

At home Suham called Nisreen and asked what food she planned on serving her guests. Nisreen recited the menu in detail.

"Is that all?" Suham asked after her daughter had finished.

"Well, yes," Nisreen stammered. "Isn't it enough?"

"Curry potatoes, rice, chicken legs and *dolemma* could feed fifteen people, of course – had not half of them been men."

"But see, I'm afraid if I make more, it'll all go to waste." Nisreen gave her opinion in her usual gentle manner. She'd inherited her easiness from her father and her beauty from her mother.

"It would be better to have leftovers rather than running low on food and seeming inconsiderate." She meant to say cheap, not inconsiderate, but since her bluntness often got her in trouble, she was as careful with her words as an attorney. "Besides, *habbibti*, would it really hurt to add a tray of shish kebab?"

"The kebabs are frozen."

"How about a roast or *kubba*?"

"It's sort of too late for a roast, and I don't know about *kubba*."

There was a pause between them. True it was too late for a roast. But *kubba*, a bulgur pie with a minced meat and onion stuffing, having been prepared months ago and placed in the freezer, need only to be defrosted and then boiled or fried in a large pan.

Since Nisreen's resistance was unusually strong this afternoon, Suham had to draw a picture of the situation with crayons. "*Habbibti*, dinner parties leave an impression on the lady of the house and the man of the house, as well as the lady of the house's mother."

"Um-hum."

"It reflects on the entire family's hospitality. So to jeopardize the family's image that way is – well, unnecessary."

"I'm not old enough for all that."

"You are married, aren't you?"

Nisreen sighed. "Okay, what if I buy cream chops from Sahara?"

Suham pondered on that a little. Feeding people restaurant food was telling them they were a nuisance. "I'll make you a roast, *habbibti*, don't worry about it."

"You're already making the *dolemma*, Mom. I don't want you to do more."

"It won't be any trouble." But trouble it was. From this point forward, the argument which originated from shish kebabs, a roast and *kubba* stretched to more sensitive issues; like the time Suham was against Nisreen going out with a Chaldean boy because he took her to see a Tom Cruise movie in the theater instead of taking her to a respectable Italian restaurant.

"It didn't matter where he would've taken me," Nisreen said, "I would've been respectful and re-spected."

"I never said you weren't respectful. I just thought he wasn't mature."

Suham thought her daughter, although married, was still a child. She should know it was as natural for a mother to worry as it was for a girl to gossip; especially here where the news was an over-protective mother, warning everyone to look out all the time, everywhere.

Nisreen then complained how her mother had criticized her wedding dress, saying it showed too much cleavage; and her husband's store, saying it made no profit; and her apartment, saying it should've had two bedrooms and not one.

Suham wished Nisreen hadn't picked up her father's bad habit of not getting over things, because now her mood was ruined for tonight's dinner. So she decided to stay home.

"You can't do that!" George protested, much too astounded for the occasion, Suham thought. He had so much to learn about life, such as how a parent should never allow their child to get away with talking back. She wasn't going to explain this now, because since the first time she'd given birth, he'd believed in her child-rearing methods as much as he knew how to joke. But at least he did pretend very hard to agree with her.

George begged that Suham set her pride aside, show up at the dinner party and make her daughter happy. But Suham wanted to teach Nisreen a lesson and by the same token not listen to him. So she made him go alone.

Once he left, she sat by the window and smoked one cigarette after another. Fifteen minutes later, the exact distance in time it took to drive to Nisreen's house, the telephone rang.

Suham answered the phone in the most natural manner, keeping in mind she did right by not going.

"Oh Mom..."

"Before you start, did you glaze the chicken with eggs?"

"Mom, if you don't come right now, I'll look like an ass in front of Alia!"

"Since I'm not there yet, Alia already thinks you an ass, *habbibti.*"

"Mom, I can't believe how stubborn you're being."

Suham's own mother once told her that her stubbornness measured to the size of all the oceans put together. Suham didn't know how that was a bad thing.

"Now be a good hostess, Nisreen, hang up the phone and go back to your guests."

Nisreen obeyed her mother and before Suham smoked another cigarette, the doorbell rang. It was Wadi and Michael coming to tie her up to the hood of the car and drive her to the hut, baste her with a seasoned sauce and roast her over an open fire.

Suham couldn't resist a smile.

"Come on," Wadi said, "lets go. Don't act as bratty with us as you do with George and your children."

Michael pushed himself through the hallway and into the family room. He turned on the television and watched the Red Wings play while Wadi called Suham's behavior childish, mean and intolerable.

Suham sat on the sofa, legs crossed, fingers tapping on the pillow, biting her lips, rolling her eyes,

waiting for her stubbornness to retire. It retired once
Wadi mentioned that their three brothers' wives,
especially Alia, suspected a rumble bigger than wres-
tling and boxing, had taken place between Suham
and Nisreen, and that they were waiting for Michael
and her to come back empty handed to confirm their
suspicions.

Suham grabbed her purse and followed Wadi to
Michael's car. Driving to Nisreen's house, Suham
got a headache listening to her sister yell at Michael
for driving too fast, stopping too abruptly, flipping off
a man who tried to pass him and turning left on a
red light. Michael didn't answer back, he just swore
beneath his breath. Wadi couldn't hear him, she was
so busy mumbling, but Suham counted over twenty
f_ _ _ words.

The minute Suham walked into Nisreen's home,
she saw her sister-in-laws' disappointment. Nisreen
instantly went to her mother, embraced and kissed
her on both cheeks. "I'm so happy you made it. You
feel okay now?"

"I wasn't really sick, *habbibti*," Suham said. "I
just had a little disagreement with your father."

She figured she'd make up a believable story of
what it was she and George disagreed about later.
She'd rather jeopardize her relationship with her
husband than that with her daughter. It was normal
for couples to disagree. And in her case, because
everyone knew how much George loved her, people
hated hearing details of their so-called problems. It'd
make them sick to know she'd done him wrong again,
and again he'd taken it.

While they gossiped and giggled, the women
leisurely prepared hors d'oeuvres. They heated four
cans of fava beans and poured lemon juice and dried

mint over them. They unwrapped the plastic foil over Alia's *houmos bil-tahine* dish and Leka's *tabbooleh* bowl. They sprinkled crisp pita bread onto Sabria's *fattoush* salad and added the garlic into the yogurt and cucumber salad. They had the younger girls do the smaller jobs, like the chips, vegetables and dip trays.

The men, in the meantime, had drinks, ate sunflower, pumpkin and watermelon seeds, pistachios and cashews, dropping half the shells on the floor and the other half on the table, even though there were three ashtrays, as they watched the Red Wings play, laughing aloud and awaiting more hors d'oeuvres.

When the ladies finished serving and finally sat down, they shared their troubles of yeast infections and backaches, they compared the elegance of one cousin's fancy wedding to another's humble one, and they discussed Iraq's horrible sanctions.

"By the way," Alia dove in the second the table was quiet (she was known to despise serious topics), "have you guys found a bride for Michael?"

"No," Suham answered, simply. If she elaborated, Alia would get a greater joy than she deserved. Any detail would bloat her heart.

Wadi, on the other hand, took the liberty of explaining how they'd considered Cousin Dalya, but the poor girl's stomach, at twenty-five, had more layers than a cabbage. And not only were Cousin Katrina's legs taller than a bed post, but she was, at twenty years old, caught with a cigarette in her mouth.

"Better in her mouth than in her ass," Alia said, eating red pistachios and laughing.

"Actually, better in her ass," Sabria, the oldest brother's wife, said, "where no one could've seen it."

Nisreen handed each one of her aunts and her mother a raspberry wine cooler and finally sat down, when everyone criticized her for working too hard.

"What about Cousin Rafida?" Nisreen asked.

"No! No!" everyone jumped at once, their complaint being that she never said hello to any body unless she was greeted first. And sometimes, she had the audacity to pretend she didn't see the person in front of her and just walked away, like a cockroach would before it could be killed.

Alia mentioned Cousin Nawal, but Hayfa said that was out of the question. "With the way she dances – all seductive – well, she couldn't possibly be a virgin."

Wadi shook her head. "These days, innocent Chaldean girls are as rare in America as baklava is in Baghdad."

A thought came to Suham, and with it, a bucket of hope and energy. She remembered a young girl she'd met in Baghdad five years ago named Rita. With the way she delicately drank her tea, turned her head and straightened her skirt, with her brown eyes, her thick hair and luscious lips, this girl had left, from that one visit, a lovely impression on Suham.

Suham hadn't considered Rita back then, since Michael was still in his twenties and in those years going back home to get married was mostly for losers. But after the Gulf War, when the number of girls wanting to flee from Iraq quadrupled and the single Chaldean ladies in America started to pursue careers or other interests, it became a trend.

Suham told Wadi and her sisters-in-law all she could remember about Rita; that she was twenty-seven now, that she had white straight teeth, a wealthy father, and three college-educated brothers. "Standing next to Michael, she'd make the most precious bride."

She paused and took a sip of her wine cooler to

allow Rita's description to settle as deeply into the women's minds as *araq*, a strong alcoholic drink made from grape juice and flavored with anise, easily would.

"Is she *Telkafia*?" Wadi asked.

"She's not from Telkaif, no. She's from Mosul."

Wadi shrugged her shoulders.

"What?" Suham said.

"She's not *Telkafia*!"

"Well, Alia is *Betnawia* and *Telkafiene* are more prejudiced toward them than they are to *Moslawiene*."

Alia dropped her eyes. Suham hadn't uttered such words to insult her sister-in-law's village, *Betnaya*, but to stop Wadi from mixing too many herbs into this topic and spoiling it. She felt bad, but not enough to do anything about it.

"She's not related," Wadi cried. "She's not *Telkafia*."

"Why must she be related?"

"I'm not saying she has to be, but it's always better than taking in a stranger."

"Not always," Leka said. "You saw what Suaad did to Imad? She turned the house upside down and threatened to divorce him if he wouldn't change all the family's stores into his name instead of having a partnership with his brothers." Her nerk came more forward. "Can you believe it?"

"What about Hania's daughter – Naeima, I think?" Alia passionately ate the pistachios, which seemed to have gotten her over any hurt feelings she'd had.

"Naeima!" Suham cried in astonishment, a bit of wine cooler leaking from the side of her mouth. "Only a fool would marry Naeima!"

Alia shrugged her shoulders. "I don't find her so horrible."

Because you are not marrying her to your brother, Suham wished to say but she'd been bad once
already. "This girl was here ages ago and she failed
the immigration test twice."

Suham gave no room for Alia to respond as she
turned quickly to Wadi. "Our relatives have disappointed Mom and Dad in Iraq, and they've disappointed us here in America – and you want to give
them someone as precious as Michael? None of them
deserve him."

"I know someone," Alia said. "But I hate getting
involved in match-making."

Oh tell, tell, everyone said, but not in those exact
words. Wadi's eyes enlarged, making Suham angry.
But she didn't show it. Instead she leaned back and
she listened to Alia's invention. Alia described a young
girl who had fish-shaped eyes, a cup-size waist, brick-
volume hair, and a dozen more qualities that made
Suham feel sicker than if she would have swallowed
lard. That woman never quit trying to cause trouble.

"Where can we see her?" Wadi asked, as excited as
a little girl who'd been given her mother's old makeup
to play with.

Alia's smile faded. "That's the thing. See, she
works in a restaurant –" And as everyone interrupted
her with their gasps, she hurried. "But not in an
Arabic one."

The stares on her didn't get any kinder. Alia
asked what was the big deal – half of America had
waitressed one time or another in their life.

"But dear sister," Hayfa said. "For an American,
it's as decent a job as being a cashier. For our people,
though, it's – well, it's just not proper."

"A Chaldean girl grows up knowing that," Suham
said, keeping herself calm. "So for her to still work
there, she's got balls. And we don't want girls with

balls."

Alia said that a cashier wasn't really in any better an environment than a waitress. Suham said that was only true in an American's eye. Alia wouldn't admit she was wrong, which outraged Suham. So she decided to put an end to this.

"If marrying a cousin in Iraq is normal, and in America it's disgusting, who can do it without shame? Us or them?"

Alia's eyes wandered from the napkins to their plates to the utensils in front of her, until her husband saved her by asking for another plate of *fattoush* salad and a bowl of fava beans. She left the table as quickly as a television was turned on. Little by little the rest of Suham's sister-in-laws scattered away from the table, as if a bomb had fallen on it. Suham was relieved to have Wadi alone.

"You were happy when Alia mentioned a strange girl, but when I brought up Rita, you completely avoided me."

"Rita is too old," Wadi said.

"She's twenty-seven, he's thirty-two. Granted, she's not young. But neither is he."

"Michael is moody," she said, reluctantly. "I don't trust him. He'll get to Baghdad and come back empty handed."

"You're making up excuses when what really bothers you is the money he'll spend with travel expenses and gifts."

Wadi seemed insulted because she jumped at the comment just as she'd jumped at the men in Baghdad who'd tasted Suham's body with their eyes. "You think I'd actually care about money when I'm marrying off my only son?"

"I know you. It's the money."

"It's not!"

"Then what?"

Wadi sat back so calmly it was as though a tranquilizer had just started working. "Well, if he goes to Baghdad, who's to go with him but me? The sanctions having cut off the food and medicine supply, conditions there are horrible. What if I have a heart attack or stroke, God forbid?"

"Cousin Badria's home has the best accommodations there. You can stay with her."

"A house won't save me. With Saddam Airport shut down, the fifteen hour drive from Jordan to Baghdad alone will kill me."

Suham thought convincing Michael to marry would be the most difficult thing of all. But Wadi was the real problem here.

"And what about you?" Wadi said. "You suddenly remember Rita and that's that. You don't want to look any more?"

"Why should I? It's torture. Either the girl is bad or her family is. Or the girl is good but ugly. Or she is pretty and good and is seventeen years old. I'm sick of it. I really am. Besides, Rita is perfect."

"No one is perfect."

"She's perfect for Michael." She frowned hard at Wadi. "What are you implying, anyway? You talk as if I'm doing this for Rita's sake and not Michael's."

"Oh please, don't be cruel. I know you love Michael, but you have to understand too – I'm scared."

"For God's sake," Suham said, irritated, "if you keep this up, we won't accomplish a thing. Make up your mind! Do you want Michael married or don't you?"

"Of course I do."

"Then stop acting like we're building a country. Chaldean women marry off their sons everyday without this much hassle."

Wadi's questions stopped all together and Suham impatiently took her bottle of wine cooler and sat next to the fireplace. This marriage wasn't going to be as pleasant as she had expected. With Wadi's paranoia, Michael's sarcasm, and everyone else's indifference towards the family's reputation, she wanted to give up as well.

Chapter 6

That week, George took Suham out to Huntington Palace, a club located on the west side, where wealthy Chaldeans met, or so they considered themselves so because they'd paid the fee of $6,000 per family for membership, plus the annual fee of $800.

Huntington Palace was tucked on top of a hill, among lots of trees. A long and narrow road, slanting way up high like a roller coaster, led to the front door where young men in black pants and vests stood with hands behind their backs, waiting to valet park the cars.

Suham thought those who established the place had two things, lots of money and misleading tongues. Not only were their fees unreasonable, but when the club was being built, they'd promised an indoor gym. All the club members got however was a pool table.

"And they've stopped sending coupon books," George had added one day, when she first complained about Huntington Palace no longer having Bingo Friday nights, something she and Wadi had enjoyed. As for the coupon books – they gave discounts to certain social functions and to elaborate dinner parties.

With no indoor gym and no Friday night Bingo, the club still remained as popular as ever, for two reasons in particular. One was the extravagant restaurant inside. Many Chaldean families enjoyed the luxury of dining out and running into people they knew. After all, being caught lingering in Huntington Palace left a good impression.

It wasn't only show offs who ate at this restaurant, of course. A lot of Chaldean businessmen met there for lunch too. And Chaldean supermarket owners were invited there by large companies like Spartan, to eat salad, shish kebab and chicken kebab, saffron rice, and sometimes, depending on the cook's mood, lentil soup.

The second reason for Huntington Palace's continuing popularity was its banquet hall, where a lot of Chaldean weddings, engagement and communion ceremonies were held. Many Middle Eastern singers on tour performed there also. Suham enjoyed attending parties there because unlike other banquet halls, its bar served her favorite drink, Pena Colada.

On Thursday night the restaurant was nearly empty, but Suham preferred it that way. The last thing she wanted was to be video taped by other men and women. She'd only come to Huntington Palace today because George was fasting and he liked the way they cooked their fish.

After George ordered his food, the waiter, whom she hadn't seen here before, turned to Suham. With his little eyes, his chunky face, and his short round body, he reminded her of Yunis Shelabi, an Egyptian comedian who was the Middle Eastern Steve Martin. As a young girl in Baghdad, she remembered the way *Mad'rest Al-Moushaghebein*, a famous old Egyptian play he was in, cleared the streets by sweeping all the people into their homes the night it was broadcast on television.

"The school of delinquents," in English, had her entire family crying with laughter.

"Do you want *tika*?" George asked.

Too preoccupied with Yunis Shelaby, she hadn't decided what she wanted to eat yet, and although grilled beef cubes on a skewer didn't sound so bad, she skimmed over the menu and ordered a steak.

"I should have been the one fasting for forty days, not you," she said as she watched the waiter place the menus underneath his arms and turn away. "At least I have a desire in my heart."

"And you think I don't?"

George probably desired that the family live healthy and be prosperous. He asked God for the same all the time, not realizing that God had fulfilled his request many years ago. God was probably getting irritated by George's near-sightedness.

"You don't need to go through the trouble of fasting," she said. "I mean you can't afford to lose an ounce."

"I can afford to, but you wouldn't like it."

She smiled. She liked it when he wasn't afraid of her. "No, I wouldn't. And do you, *habbibi*, honestly want to stack up on my disapprovals of you?"

"Is that the desire in your heart – that I change?"

She grinned. "No, I've stopped asking for that."

He stared at her hard, and her grin spread out like a tree. Regardless of what he said, she knew from his eyes that he loved her genius more than he did her heart.

"Then is it to marry Michael?"

She didn't answer and he laughed, which irritated her. But she remained civil about it, knowing that she had a tendency to become as sensitive about Michael's issues as she was about her *kiliecha*.

"I assure you that boy won't get married now."

She continued being civil, matching his impertinence. "It's my duty to see that he might."

"Give him a few more years and then try..."

"So he can be more addicted to this lifestyle?"

He shook his head while chewing a piece of bread and butter. "Everyone is addicted to something before they give it up."

She arched a brow. "Sometimes you impress me."

"Less than sometimes, unfortunately." He nodded his head, his thoughts as distant from her as hers usually were from him. "I think, concerning your nephew, it's dangerous to interfere."

"We're not talking about a gun here, *habbibi*, we're talking about my nephew's future."

He didn't respond.

"Well?" Suham was starting to enjoy this conversation as much as she did Turkish coffee, of which she always wanted refills.

"I don't know what to say."

"Why not?"

"You're the artistic one here." His tone was sarcastic but when she accused him of that, he said he was no more sarcastic than she'd been since he married her.

"Whether you know it or not, or whether you pretend you don't know it, you are the one who traps me in here," she said, pressing her finger to her head, in case he didn't understand.

"I'd like you however you are."

"I don't think so."

The waiter came and placed the salad on the table. He said he'd be back with their dinner in a few minutes.

George started in on his salad. "My brother asked us to visit him in California this summer. His son is taking communion."

Wait a minute, she thought. Where did George go? She wanted powerful words to continue falling from his lips.

"Fadi could run the store since he'll be on school break."

"I don't know, George. Michael might get married this summer."

"He might is one thing and he will is another."

This time she didn't restrain herself and asked him not to mention Michael's name for the rest of the night. She suddenly considered getting away for a while, somewhere much further than Wadi's house and longer than a Saturday night.

The waiter came again and saved George from the brutal words brewing inside Suham. He cleared the table of empty salad plates and then placed the entrees in front of Suham and George. The process took only a few minutes but it gave Suham a chance to pack her anger a lunch bag and send it off to her kidneys until the school bus came to pick it up.

The waiter asked if they'd like anything else.

"No, thank you," they both responded.

George started eating the fish. "If Michael does marry, that's even better. You'll have two parties to go to this summer."

Fixing the situation now was like stopping the war after the missiles were shot. "I can think of four other parties we'll be invited to."

"But they're not our immediate family. They don't concern us the same way."

"You're right, but that's not the point."

"What is it then?"

She looked at her steak but her hands remained on her lap. "I don't want to go."

"Why not?" he asked, not once, not twice, but

three times. All three times she refused to answer. She didn't want to be the cold-hearted one. She knew how to love deeply, even though she didn't do it with a smile on her face.

"Why?" she heard a fourth time.

"Because, if you must press me into saying it, Salem isn't a good brother." She took a deep breath. "He really doesn't deserve us to fly to California and make him feel proud and important in front of his wife and business partners." She didn't include friends in this speech because surely no one would want to associate themselves with a man as greedy as Salem. She spared George that fact.

"Alright, alright."

"Oh, you stir up my emotions and end it there?"

"Well, what do you want me to say?" he said. "I mean the man is not wicked."

Frowning, her lips twitched in disgust. "You really are simple minded."

Those words had slipped out of her mouth like a wet fish once had out of her hands. George bent his head, as if he'd just been given holy bread and was walking away from the altar. To camouflage the boldness of her insult, Suham didn't let that be her last comment.

"I mean does someone have to be wicked before you draw the line?"

He didn't defend his brother or himself and his silence irritated her skin worse than ants had once done in Baghdad when they'd climbed her little thighs and entered her underwear. Things would be so much easier if he spoke of and cared about parrots or tangerines instead of her only.

"I have a favor to ask of you," she said, bravely.

He lifted his eyes to her.

"I need you to call your cousin in Baghdad for me.

But I don't want you to ask me any questions yet."

"Then what would I say to her?"

"I'll do all the talking. You must only greet her, as she is, you know, your cousin."

George wore his glasses and searched for his cousin's number through the Virginia Slims telephone book the cigarette company had given him as a promotion many years ago. Meanwhile, Suham smoked a cigarette and paced back and forth. George dialed and re-dialed Fatin's number for over an hour, but the telephone lines to Baghdad were busy.

He got through after five hours. He briefly greeted his cousin before handing Suham the phone, in case the lines got disconnected, something which, since the war, normally happened after three or five minutes, depending on the Iraqi operator's mood.

Suham asked Fatin if her neighbor Rita had married and when she received "No" as an answer, she revealed her intentions; that she was interested in Rita as Michael's future bride. Fatin encouraged the idea, saying Rita was lovely, like Michael, whom she assumed to be of the highest respectability and honor, being of Suham's blood and heritage. Rita deserved the very best. She offered to introduce them to each other through pictures and appraisals.

"Before the lines cut off, tell me how are you doing?" Suham asked, now that her business was done. She spoke clearly and loudly because sometimes – this being one of them – Iraqi telephone lines had more static than a radio without an antenna.

"We're doing fine," Fatin said, with a somber voice, though. "*Allah kareem.*"

God is generous, one of the Middle East's favorite sayings. Fatin had said it whole-heartedly, even though circumstances in Iraq were unbearable.

Suham missed being a part of that religious group, where the word God was said as often there as "I love you" was here. It was used, with no discrimination or exaggeration, everywhere; at tea parties and during wedding ceremonies, at funerals and during illness and hospital visits.

Fatin assured Suham she would visit Rita and give her the message after she finished frying the meat and tomatoes that sat on the skillet over the fire, but definitely before she hung the laundry outside. The ladies gave each other Arabic blessings and said their goodbyes.

Suham felt melancholy afterwards. Hanging up the phone had been easy, but forgetting Fatin's voice wouldn't be. She was touched by her contentment.

"Why couldn't you tell me your plan to begin with?" George asked.

"You would've discouraged me."

"I would have tried, but I wouldn't have succeeded."

"Then I spared you the time."

He placed himself beneath the covers, and she got into bed beside him. He'd done a superb job of being patient. She rolled her hair around her ear and smiled at him. "Do you love me?"

"You know I do."

"Despite everything –"

"Despite what?"

"Whatever it is you think I do to you."

"I don't think that way and you know it. You're the one who knows it."

"Knows what I do to you?"

"Knows everything!"

She smiled and came near him. He wrapped her in his arms and kissed her hard. With deep breaths, he drank her aura as if it was a cold glass of pomegranate juice.

Those days came for Suham as often as a house-wife broke an egg on the kitchen floor, but when they did happen their power kept her from losing her sweetness altogether and becoming bitter.

Chapter 7

Suham waited for her husband to leave for work the following morning, so he'd stop kissing her naked shoulders and smelling her unwashed hair. Her thoughts about Michael's wedding did not want to be disturbed.

George touched her nightgown's thin straps and stared at them with interest. "Do you want anything from the store?"

She didn't want a single thing, but not to hurt his feelings, she thought of a food she'd craved but hadn't had in a while. "What I want is not in your store, *habbibi*."

"I'll drive anywhere..."

"Are you sure?"

"I'm positive."

"Then two *shawarma* sandwiches from Beirut Palace."

He kissed her shoulders hard, as if thanking her for being so kind as to let him buy her some treats. She smiled and looked at him. "Must you kiss me so much?"

"You don't like it?"

"I love it," she said. "But I don't deserve it really. I hate feeling guilty."

"If anyone should feel guilty, it should be me."

"Because you don't understand me?"

"Because I enjoy it so much."

Her smile widened. "Oh."

The minute the front door slammed shut, Suham raised the blinds and prepared her ritual of Turkish coffee and a cigarette. But she didn't take the usual route down memory lane this morning. She was planning a trip to Baghdad to visit Rita's patio instead. The packing took nearly ten minutes, but the flight only a second.

In her mind, Suham arrived safely to a picture of two cups of mint tea steaming and dozens of birds chirping and orange blossoms blossoming and delicate wind flowing, and in the center of it all, two women talking about a delicious subject, marriage – before it happened, of course (when else was marriage as delicious).

While Fatin laughed and teased, Rita sat with legs crossed and a shy smile. She'd suspect that the loneliness of a decade would be ending soon, because the man she'd turned down many suitors for had come. Her mother was wrong all along. She shouldn't have married Mr. Rich or Mr. Cousin. People were wrong too. She wasn't too picky or too heartless.

The aura of this scene was as close to Suham's heart as the gold necklace around her neck.

Suham kept the call she'd made to Baghdad a secret from Wadi, because Wadi wanted to first consider other Chaldean girls before resorting to a less convenient marriage. Suham agreed. She figured that once Rita's pictures arrived, everyone would cooperate.

So Suham called Hassina, an old Chaldean cousin of her deceased mother, and through her, was updated on who'd gotten married, who'd gotten divorced, who'd been unfaithful. Suham put up with thirty minutes of gossip, but the results were useful, leading to three possible brides.

Suham crossed the first two out because they were under nineteen. The third girl, on the other hand, named Dunia, sounded suitable enough to look into. Hassina didn't have enough information on Dunia, but her cousin-in-law's daughter did. So Suham called her.

She found out that Dunia was not fat or skinny but "proportionate", had red hair, was twenty-six and worked at a supermarket in Detroit. She told Suham the name of the supermarket and asked her not to mention she'd been the source, because her husband didn't like her meddling in this type of business.

Suham planned on visiting Dunia right away, but when Michael heard about it, he was outraged.

"Who said I don't want to marry a young girl?" He was referring to the first two girls Hassina had mentioned and whom Wadi had told him about.

"I'm sure you want just that," Suham said. "But nowadays, unless she's in love with you, no eighteen year old girl will accept a man your age. And if she does, there's something wrong with her."

"Where did you get that idea – from Hassina's gossip?" His eyes were furious, as though he was fighting for a girl he'd courted for years. "My friend Sahir married a girl fifteen years younger than him."

"From here?"

"From Baghdad!"

"Well, we're not in Baghdad, where any girl will take any man to come to America and live rich. Here they're already rich."

His eyes calmed a little, but his temper was still as hot as pepper. "I want to see them, anyway."

"Michael, must you put us in awkward positions

before you figure out what you want won't do?"

"What about Ala' – his wife was barely sixteen!"

"Even if you want a sixteen year old girl, we don't," she said, firmly, seeing that he wasn't getting the point. "A young girl will love you today and five years from now, she'll hate you for disrupting her youth." She should know.

Michael raged about how his aunt didn't under-stand life because she lived at home all day long. As he cussed and shouted, Suham watched him with sympathetic eyes, seeing that this boy knew nothing at all about love and marriage.

She didn't want him to leave her house with hurt feelings, so she spent hours convincing him that nineteen-year-old girls weren't mature enough to satisfy someone like him, who was experienced and distinguished in life. And besides, twenty-six wasn't old. She'd still be six years younger than him. He should give Dunia a chance. "She may surprise you, Michael."

He agreed, but on the condition that he alone visited the supermarket first. Suham didn't trust Michael's judgement: he knew as much about pick-ing a good girl as he did about picking a watermelon. But she told him to do as he liked.

"I'll arrange it for you to see her this coming week then," she said.

Suham called the supermarket that afternoon and asked for directions. Then she requested Dunia's work schedule.

"Dunia is right here," the man on the other end of the line said. "If you'd like, you can ask her your-self."

He didn't give her a chance to say she preferred to get the information from him, and within seconds she heard, "Hello", in a pleasant voice.

Suham greeted Dunia warmly and asked how she was doing before introducing the intentions of her call: that some good people had directed her to Dunia, and they wished to come to the supermarket and get acquainted.

"You're welcome to do so, of course," Dunia said. Then she asked who those good people were. Suham said they wished to stay anonymous.

So Dunia read her week's schedule. Monday, Tuesday, and Thursday from eight to three. Wednesday, Friday and Saturday from two to nine. And every other Sunday, from nine to two. She then paused, as if awaiting her teacher to correct her grammar.

Suham thanked Dunia for her time and apologized if she'd taken her away from work. "Well, then, if God is willing, may we see each other this week."

"Yes, if God is willing."

Michael went to the supermarket a few days later. Suham occupied herself with slicing zucchini rings, chopping onions and pealing tomatoes for that day's stew while she waited to hear Michael's impressions, which Michael had promised to deliver from his cellular phone.

"I didn't know which one she was," he said when he called.

The bowl of onions she was ready to throw over the sizzling meat was suspended in the air. "The one with red hair!"

"They all had red hair."

"Oh, Michael." The hissing in the pot grew louder, and she lowered the stove's temperature and added the onions.

"Anyway, it doesn't matter which one she was because they were all ugly."

The next day, Suham had George drive her and Wadi to see Dunia since the supermarket's neighborhood was too dangerous for women to go to alone. It being a feminine matter, George waited in the car as the two sisters walked through the building's barred fence, their postures as straight as bookbindings and their faces as serious as the Iraqi principles, known for their strictness.

The supermarket had five narrow aisles, four registers and four cashiers, all of whom had red hair, from strawberry to carrot.

Suham's eyes quickly searched for the most proportionately sized cashier, unable to bear the smell of spoiled pork and rotting tomatoes. But Michael was right. None were pretty. Neither were they proportionate.

"It's none of them," she told Wadi.

"How do you know?"

"It can't be – that one is at least forty, that one is fat, the other two can't be more than seventeen."

Suham impatiently approached one of the cashiers and asked if she could direct her to Dunia. The girl looked at Suham like she knew exactly what was taking place, not that it was a mystery. Two overdressed Chaldean women, looking lost and being in a hurry couldn't mean anything but that they were bride-hunters.

"Dunia is on her break in the back room."

With Wadi in her wake, Suham hurried in that direction, past the meat counters. They saw a butcher rearranging pork chop packages and asked if he could tell Dunia she had visitors. He went slowly into the back room, and Suham and Wadi squeezed themselves against Pepsi cartons to make way for customers to pass their shopping carts through the aisle.

"Let me do the talking," Suham said.

Dunia came out five minutes later, and Suham regretted that she had delayed cooking her cauliflower stew and washing the bed sheets for her. It wasn't that Dunia was ugly, as Michael had pronounced all the girls in the supermarket to be, but her hair was short, hard, and of two colors, the roots plum and the rest golden.

Dunia invited them into the back. Cases of empty Pepsi, Coke, and Faygo bottles were stacked up against the walls. Dunia's lunch, a bag of McDonalds', sat on top of cardboard boxes. She asked a man to bring milk cartons for Suham and Wadi to sit on.

He did as she'd asked. Wadi gladly sat but Suham thanked Dunia's hospitality and said she'd rather stand. She had her nice jacket on and the cartons were filthy. Dunia prepared coffee, one with cream for Suham, one cream and one spoon of sugar for Wadi, and served it to them with a wide smile.

The three of them chatted about everything but the reason behind the visit. Suham didn't even introduce themselves to Dunia, knowing that their acquaintance would end here.

After this unprofitable attempt, Suham inquired about good girls through other sources. But they too were of no help; they either mentioned more unsuitable girls or they said they knew of no one at the time but promised to keep their eyes open. For a few weeks, Suham had no feedback.

Then one day Itaf, the electrolysist, called with some news. A twenty-four year old manicurist. Not a prestigious job, but the more difficult it was to find a good girl, the less picky Suham was becoming.

"Make an appointment with her to get your nails done," Itaf said. "She works out of her home."

Suham's eppointment was Tuesday and when Linda opened the door, her smile was as dressed up as a porcelain doll. She was dressed simply in jeans and a black shirt, but she was far from that. Clothes aside, the girl consisted of saffron colored hair that hung down to her tiny waist. It was puffed up, permed, colored, teased and gorgeous. Her rose lipstick, thick mascara and green contacts were sure to scare off every arranged marriage proposal.

With piano-like fingers and long pink nails, Linda's touch was as delicate as a summer's breeze, and as wonderful. Her perfume blew towards Suham every time she moved her hands to grab a nail file or return a liquid bottle of nail hardener on the table. She was as nervous as she was pretty. And she worked hard at keeping her good posture and smile. There were two children in the house, her nephews. They kept trying to get their aunt's attention but failed repeatedly. She was busy trying to impress Suham.

"I write poetry."

Suham nodded her head, but didn't smile. "Very nice."

"I love reading books too."

One of her nephews climbed over the kitchen's railing, which partially separated the kitchen from the family room. Linda stared at him with vicious eyes and ordered him to stop. He wouldn't listen and she began fidgeting in her seat.

Suham said she thought the boy adorable and didn't mind him playing around them. The boy finally stopped climbing and came to stand beside Linda.

"Go sit over there!" she demanded. She caught herself then, adding, "*Habbibi.*"

"You know, Itaf is the one who sent me to you," Suham said to distract Linda from the little boy.

Linda's eyes lit up like a rocket. "Oh, isn't she

wonderful? She did my whole body – stomach and all!"

Wadi had furnished the table with a pot of cardamom tea and a plate of Spanish cheese with sliced cucumbers, tomatoes, black olives and parsley. She was expecting Suham to come after she'd got her nails done.

"I'm starving so don't ask questions until I've eaten," Suham said.

Wadi catered to Suham as if she had just given birth. The only thing Suham had to do was roll pita bread over slices of cheese and tomatoes and eat while drinking tea.

"Now, you can ask me whatever you like."

"No point in doing that," Wadi said. "If it was good news, you would have told me from the front door."

"Don't lose all hope from now. Sometimes people go through years of hunting before finding a bride."

"Other people are stronger than me. I've barely survived the headache of the past couple of months."

Suham told her every detail, how the girl wore green contacts and had electrolysis done on her entire body, including her stomach. Wadi gasped or shook her head to each description.

"Girls here have changed," Suham said. "You can't please them and they can't please you."

Wadi nodded her head and sighed. Suham was itching to bring up Rita's name. She'd hoped Wadi would do it first, but it was ridiculous to rely on Wadi for anything. "I don't see why you dread the thought of – oh, forget it."

"Oh, Suham!"

"Don't worry, I won't mention her name."

"Go ahead and mention it. God knows you want to."

"Do you blame me?"

Wadi whimpered something about her bad luck.

Suham leaned forward and looked closely at Wadi. "I'm starting to think you don't want this girl just because I do."

"That's ridiculous! Don't be cruel." Then Wadi mumbled something about how terrible a son Michael was, and how difficult he'd been from birth.

Suham saw Wadi really was scared. She probably thought they were going to smuggle cocaine into Iraq, not marry Michael off. "Trust me, Rita is someone you'd like," she gently assured her sister. "And so would Michael."

"What if he goes all the way to Baghdad and it doesn't work out?"

"That wouldn't be the end of the world, would it? It'll be like a vacation."

"But Iraq is an awful place right now."

"People go there everyday…"

"They'll give him a hard time because he's an Arabic man with an American passport. You know them."

Suham placed her chin over her fist and looked at the ceiling. "Men go to Iraq to find brides everyday and they come back safe, but once Wadi's son gets there, all hell will break loose. Bombs will explode, missiles will take off, the war will start all over again."

"Michael is my only son and I'll die if anything happens to him."

Suham stroked her finger around the cup's rim as she searched for a solution. If anything were to happen to Michael, she'd die to.

"I have an idea," she said with her genius smile. "We'll ask Rita to meet you half-way, like in Jordan maybe."

That idea pleased Wadi as much as it would've

Alia. Instead of cheering up, she complained about the world having drastically changed since she was a girl.

"What now?" Suham demanded.

Wadi quit her moaning and raised her head as high as an ostrich. "Do you realize how much this will all cost?"

Suham was dumbfounded. Did this woman really share a house with Michael? "Your son throws his money on girls like he's throwing bread for birds. At least when he's married, his money will go to a wife and not whores."

Wadi's face suddenly turned from a heavy dough to a warm broth, which led Suham to believe the wedding she'd been trying to arrange for months was within reach, just as the Spanish cheese on the table.

Chapter 8

The marriage topic was dropped until Rita's pictures arrived in the mail one afternoon. Suham tore the envelope and took a good look at them before calling Michael and asking him to dinner with her and George.

"I have a surprise for you," she said.

"What, *kuzzi?*"

"I cooked *ras asfoor* today, sorry, but I'll be sure to make you a stuffed lamb next time."

Suham had always believed that *ras asfoor*, bird's head, was a dish named by a mischievous boy who climbed over people's fences and stole peaches off their trees, since only he would be creative enough to give the meatballs in the potato stew that label.

Today Suham spent less time setting the table with side dishes because she kept going back to look at Rita's pictures. She sat on the couch and scrutinized them proudly, as if she were personally responsible for Rita's beauty.

And when she, with utmost confidence, placed the pictures in Michael's hand that night as he and George drank tea and dipped ripe dates into yogurt, she was delighted to see him enjoy them as much as she had.

But within seconds, a smile escaped his lips, and she steeled herself. "Is this the surprise?"

"It's easy for you to say that, of course," she said. "You didn't walk through the jungle that Wadi and I walked through to find the tiger."

"I did so," he defended himself. "What about the red head?"

"Well, there you are!"

He looked at the picture again. "I have to get to know her first."

"That goes without saying."

"I don't want to get involved with a girl without dating her for a while," he repeated, but grinning this time. "And risk ending up like you two."

Suham took a long look at George, and seeing that tonight, he'd be as absorbent to her teasing as a sponge, she puckered her lips and raised her chin a few inches, a posture that she knew he adored even more than her voluptuousness.

"It's not how we got married that's the problem," she said, "it's that my husband loves me when I'm cruel and gets confused when I'm nice."

George studied her harder than he did his store's cigarette inventory list. She smiled devilishly, raised her chin another inch and then turned to Michael. "I have her phone number. If you'd like, I'll introduce you."

They shook hands on it, and went their separate ways – Suham to the dirty dishes, Michael to God knows where. She was so happy with the outcome that if Lisa appeared unexpectedly at her doorsteps, Suham would welcome her with a kiss on each cheek.

Not only did the phone call take place, but it lead to many others. And like a girl who had difficulty stopping a boy she desired to be touched by as much as he desired to touch, Michael no longer resisted marriage. This gave way for Suham to elaborate on the wedding details without his sarcasm. Nowadays when she spoke, he listened, and willingly, as though she was discussing the Red Wings' play offs.

"Girls treasure jewelry from birth," Suham said when she and Wadi talked and joked about how Michael had changed. "But the only time a man cares about it is when he finds a gem with firm breasts and a good behind."

The number of Michael's calls to Rita – five a week – worried Wadi, since she figured the telephone bill would come to the price of two plane tickets, and it surprised the rest of the family.

"When he's home now, he looks like he belongs here," Wadi said to Suham. "Before, he used to fidget a thousand times, like a snake lived inside of him."

Suham corrected her and said that it wasn't a snake alone, but the entire wilderness population. Not that that was a bad thing. She too had the same illness inside. The difference was that she didn't have the same symptoms.

Suham called Fatin and thanked her for all the trouble she had taken. She then bought her gifts; log-sleeved, below the knee dresses for her and her two daughters, an autumn wool jacket for her husband and some cheap makeup. She'd send the gifts with Wadi to Jordan, and from there, Rita's mother would deliver them to Baghdad.

Then Suham called Rita for the last procedure, to ask for her weight, height, birth date, and dress size, to avoid a scam. If any detail had been tampered with, Michael's family had every right, religiously, to pull out.

Suham also kept her promise to Wadi and told Rita how meeting in Amman, rather than in Baghdad, would be more convenient for both parties. She and Michael had already gotten acquainted and they couldn't marry in Baghdad anyway, with Iraqi law against its citizens immigrating to another country. So, since she must marry in Jordan either way, it would be a waste of time for Michael to travel the long distance just to escort her out of Iraq.

"Besides, Rita, *habbibti*, Michael can't afford too much time away from his store," Suham lied, figuring that once Michael married, he'd turn into a true businessman anyway.

To all this, Rita agreed as beautifully as a bird sang, with ease.

Just then the Iraqi law – it changed everyday – was that a girl couldn't leave her country unless escorted by a male relative. Since her father was deceased and her mother being under fifty, wasn't legally old enough to take on that role single-handedly, and her brothers were too young to be given permission to leave the country, her uncle took on that duty.

Suham suggested that Rita, her mother and her uncle, take the bus to Jordan three days before Michael left Detroit, in case problems arose with the Iraqi authorities and their trip was somehow delayed. Of course, problems from here would never occur, as long as Michael and Wadi made it to the airport before the flight took off.

Rita understood and again she agreed. Suham also explained that the wedding ceremony and *el-seigha*, the dressing of the bride with gold, would await her, the bride, in America. Rita understood that as well and said she hadn't expected it any other way.

"You are getting married, dear," Suham said. "*Fa itjahezi.*"

Rita said of course she'd also prepare her dowry of gold, clothes and gifts.

Suham quickly moved on to the next issue, the wedding ceremony. Although she'd done this before with Nisreen, she was no expert at it, because with her daughter, Suham was the makeup artist on the movie set, not the director. In the Chaldean and Arabic tradition, the man's side of the family paid for the wedding and so had the privilege of preparing it. Of course, brides who lived in America gave their opinion and negotiated certain details, but unless she was asking for trouble, she did not expect to have the last word.

Suham, as close to the groom's side as a pistachio was to its shell, took on the first task, making appointments with three Chaldean florists who worked out of their homes. She and Wadi visited Layla first, the most popular of the three. Layla lived two miles south of Suham, in a small home with gorgeous landscaping. The trees and bushes looked like they'd just came out of a barber's shop. The patio had two wicker chairs with a table between them.

Suham stared at the scenery and wished she had taken up an interest beyond her regular duties of cleaning, of cooking, of sitting on the couch with a cup of Turkish coffee in her hand and a cigarette in her mouth, of looking out the window and yearning to be sixteen again.

Layla seated them in the guestroom, or what it should be called, the Orient. Aside from the fake flower arrangements and tulle tucked in the corner, the room had as much Chinese furniture and paintings as her garden had flowers.

Layla asked her children in the next room to lower the TV volume as she walked to the kitchen. There were photo albums of Chaldean parties Layla

had been hired to do and magazines of floral arrangements on top of the center table for her customers.
Suham and Wadi flipped through them. They complimented her work when she returned with an Oriental
tray of tea.

While Wadi drank her tea, Suham described
their circumstances. They planned on having her
nephew's wedding reception at Biondo's, an Italian
banquet hall on the east side, and that they wanted a
simple centerpiece.

"Yes, we don't want anyone fighting over it," Wadi
said, then told of an experience she had once had at
a communion party, where the centerpiece at each
table was a statue of Jesus' head, and having sat
down first, she'd assumed it went to her. Then a lady
appeared and claimed she'd reserved the table a half-
an-hour earlier.

"'See, my sister?' she said to me and held up her
purse," Wadi said. "She had it sitting on the chair,
but I didn't see it! I let her have the statue, of course,
but if it was someone else –" She closed her eyes and
shook her head. "Hmm!"

Layla excused herself and returned to the kitch-
en, and Suham and Wadi put their heads together
and searched the photo albums more intently. When
she came back with a plate of spinach and meat pies
and a plate of *kiliecha*, Suham pointed out what they
wanted in one of the photo albums. A burgundy thick-
shaped candle with a base of flowers and leaves. The
guests would light the candles before the best man
made the toast, and the candle would remain lit until
after the bridal dance.

Layla wrote the details down on a small yellow
pad and Suham continued with the rest of the order.
For the bridal tables' background, window-shaped
boxes with silver drapery; tulle crossing the dance

floor's ceiling, with fake doves hanging from it; six tall poles, wrapped with tulle and bright lights, lined up near the main entrance; a train of flowers attached to the edge of the bridal party table and the cake table.

"What about the bouquets?" Layla asked.

"We're bringing the girl from Iraq and since she has no relatives here," Suham said, "we're just having a maid-of-honor and a best man."

Layla said that was appropriate, because most Chaldean men who married back home didn't have as elaborate a wedding as those who married in America.

Layla went over the list she'd written on the pad. "What about an arm ribbon for the groom?"

"We already have an arm ribbon." Suham wasn't going to have Wadi pay seventy some dollars for a decoration that no one, maybe not even a priest, knew what it symbolized. She'd just use the ribbon Nisreen's husband married in.

Layla quoted them for $2600 for everything, which changed to $2000 after much bargaining and tea drinking. Suham asked whether the wedding date not having been set would cause any problems. Layla assured them she'd manage fine if given a month's notice.

"Once Rita is handed her visa," Suham said, "we'll start making reservations."

They departed after everything was agreed upon, but to make sure Layla's work and prices were reasonable, Suham and Wadi visited the other florists as well. Those visits were brief, however, because one woman charged as high as a florist using fresh flowers would, while the other's work was as unprofessional as a homemade birthday cake.

"Pick the cake however you want it," Wadi said to

Suham as they, along with Nisreen, went down the list
of what needed to be done now and what could wait
until later. "But please, nothing too big and gaudy."

"You'll be back in time for that," Suham said. "It's
only Rita who'll be stuck in Jordan."

The wedding would be held at Biondo's, but not
too many people would be invited – four hundred,
four-fifty, the most. The dinner would consist of the
usual soup and salad, and for the main entrée, a plate
of chicken and steak with vegetables and a potato.
Then for dessert, a bowl of ice cream.

By next month, they'd hire Heaven's Band, since
these days the more famous King's Band charged
$2000 to perform in wedding parties. And anyway,
Heaven Band had done a good job in Nisreen's wedding. For photography and video taping, they'd hired
Imad Savaya, the best in the Chaldean community,
asking him to use two, not one, cameras.

The wedding arrangements were not discussed
with Michael because as with most men, Arabic or
American, he didn't care. He occasionally heard
which banquet hall the wedding reception would be
held in or who'd be the maid-of-honor, and sometimes
Suham tried to get him involved, but his only comment would be, "Just keep it under $30,000 and I'll
be happy."

Suham did not question Michael about Rita,
thinking it a private matter now that the two were in
some form of a relationship. But when one day he
called and invited himself for lunch, she, knowing
that he wanted to speak of the matter, was delighted,
excited, and impatient to have him to herself.

She hadn't planned on cooking dinner that
night, so it was too late to defrost the meat for any
stew. Michael wasn't a meat fanatic, but the only
stews that tasted decent without meat were white

beans and sometimes cauliflower. And even those two meals were never cooked vegetarian unless it was lent. Thinking of the easiest recipe at such short notice, Suham decided on frying small beef slices with tomatoes.

She didn't serve Michael the food in a dish but left it in the pan, so the tomato sauce, with the delicious burnt flavor, would be scraped off the bottom with pita bread. She placed a bowl of parsley and a cup of tea beside the pan. Michael complained he wanted Pepsi.

His request was as weird as if he had asked for a watermelon with his meal. "Tea goes better with beef and tomatoes, *habbibi*."

He obediently drank the tea and quietly ate his food. Suham was curious about his behavior, wondering whether it was a sign of maturity or a problem. But she pretended not to notice, asking about his work and his friends, but nothing else.

"I like the way Rita doesn't make a big deal out of things," he said, after he'd finished telling her that his uncle was running the business as well as his father had. "She's really understanding."

Suham grinned. "You've had your first fight?"

"No, but when I told her how I feel – that I'm only coming to Jordan to meet her, you know, nothing more," he said in a casual manner, "she said that was fine. It might not work out, I told her. She said that was fine too, and I liked that. She thinks the same way I do."

Suham was confused. He talked as though backing out of an engagement would be as easy as backing out of a driveway.

"You know, we meet and talk and see how things are going," he continued to explain like a philosopher, seeming very pleased, even proud of his theory, although it was disturbing Suham a great deal. "And we'll deal with the rest later."

"Of course," Suham agreed, restraining herself. She had been under the wrong impression all along. She'd thought Michael knew what he was doing. He knew nothing.

"I mean we might not get along or I might not feel chemistry with her..." He went on and on about the same thing. Suham's head was so foggy she couldn't make out his speech clearly. But this much she understood; that Michael would basically throw away Rita as quickly as a grenade, if he felt like it.

Suham looked deeply at him, unable to move, unable to speak. Something about him frightened her. She thought it best to brush the subject aside, until she was better equipped to handle it.

And maybe this was just a stupid talk. If Rita's pictures alone had touched his heart enough to consider going to Jordan, then what would standing face to face with her do?

Chapter 9

Once Suham booked the flight tickets (she was the only one she could depend on for finding the lowest fares and for giving the correct spelling of Michael's last name) Wadi held a party for Michael. They gave Rita the exact day of the party, so that her family could have one in her honor on the same day.

At Suham's nagging, Wadi bought a stuffed lamb. Suham's reasoning was that since Michael didn't have an engagement ceremony, this party would be a substitute, and it must be handled just as honorably. After giving into the lamb principle, Wadi asked Suham to bake her a cake.

Suham was too tired to argue that serving Betty Crocker to her guests, particularly on this occasion, would conflict with the extravagance of the lamb, so she agreed. But behind Wadi's back, she special ordered a cake from the Middle Eastern Bakery. The rest of the cooking was distributed amongst Suham, Nisreen and the sisters-in-law.

Suham had volunteered to make a roast and a *tabbooleh*. The roast was easy, but the *tabbooleh* was energy consuming. She had to rinse the bulgur, dice the tomatoes, slice the onions, dunk bunches of parsley into the water, swing them back and forth outside to dry, cut off their stalks, chop the parsley and mint thin, add the salt, squeeze the lemons, pour the olive oil, mix it with the hands, set it aside, let the bulgur absorb the tomato juice and soften, rest a while and return to it half-an-hour later.

It was always the sight of the *tabbooleh*, completed, that erased the fatigue it had caused a woman, a little the way a baby's face made a mother forget her labor and had her saying, "I'd do it all over again."

Suham went early to Wadi's house, so she could help set up the seeds, nuts and hors d'oeuvres in the appropriate bowls, trays and dishes. Wadi took out Rita's pictures from the kitchen cupboards. She placed one over the television set, another on the living room table and a third on the kitchen counter. There was little to drink in the bar, so Suham asked George to bring the liquor, since she didn't know where Michael was and preferred not to rely on him.

The ladies then sat in the patio while awaiting everyone else's arrival. They had front-row seats to Wadi's vegetable garden, which consisted of peppermint leaves, hot and mild peppers, tomatoes, cucumbers and beets. Thinking it as chaotic as the guest-room upstairs, Suham tried to change the garden's arrangements every spring. But Wadi wouldn't have it, saying it'd be like letting a relative meddle in her husband's underwear drawer.

"If she'll do a better job, why not?" Suham had said.

They watched an orange moon rise so gracefully from behind two trees, it looked like God was pulling it by a string, telling it to come and eat supper. God seemed to be right on schedule when it came to the sun, moon and stars, as though He were their school bus. She wondered if He'd run out of gas by the time He reached earth, therefore often arriving late, and that that was why "good things came to those who waited."

The peaceful moment on the patio ended when cars started to park in the driveway. The children started their mischief from outside the house as they tampered with Wadi's mailbox and her doorbell.

When George came, Suham rushed him to the guestroom and asked him to set the liquor on the bar table. He smelled of beer and she asked him why that was.

"We caught a shoplifter today. A beef jerky."

She put her hands up for him to stop. "*Habbibi*, I don't want to hear about you having jeopardized your life for a beef jerky."

"He didn't fight, though!"

She kissed him on the cheek. "Why don't you go sit with the men and I'll make you a plate of hors d'oeuvres."

He rubbed his chin while turning his head to the family room, where the men laughed loudly. He smiled kindly at her and seemed to use as much energy walking away as he would to push a car.

She wished he ran any other business but a party store. At times his job seemed more dangerous than that of a police officer. But the store made more profit for the family than any desk job could, and he had operated in this one and only field for over twenty years.

Michael was the last guest to appear, causing a ruckus. The men clapped and cheered him on, as if he was a football player who just had scored a touch down. The women *helhelou* by placing one hand over the lip, and with the tongue, making an Arabic mirth. Although it was used on all happy occasions, this gesture was most popular during weddings; was usually, but not always, performed by married women, and was done for people closely related. Women often competed amongst themselves to have the loudest or most pleasant *helhoula*, the act itself.

Everyone greeted Michael with hugs and kisses and congratulations. The men returned to their game and liquor until the women started dancing in front of the TV to Kathim Al-Sahir songs, the most popular singer in all the Middle East. His Iraqi lyrics turned smoke into perfume and salt into sugar, and his voice was sweeter than baklava.

After a little bit of dancing Suham hid in Wadi's bedroom, knowing that soon dinner would be served and that once that happened, there was no escaping the greasy pots and the dozens of dishes. She'd passed by Wadi's room every weekend, but this was the first time she'd been inside for months. It smelt of incense and fresh laundry, and with the holy pictures hanging on the walls and the rosaries hanging over the pictures, it felt like a church washed with Tide.

A little breeze came through the window and the curtains flapped, like a girl's dress did in the wind. She loved its rhythmic sound, making her feel the presence of someone or something that had no name or label. She wondered if she'd let herself go, whether the wind would do to her what he did to the curtains, move her any way it liked. She wanted that, to have no say in the matter, to not arm wrestle with decisions, yet to physically move.

The door squeaked open and behind it stood Wadi. Her distraught expression told the whole story; Michael had upset her and she needed Suham to fix things. And she'd considered letting the wind run her life! No one gave her a chance to sit alone in a room while they made their own decisions.

"He says, `Just because I'm going to Jordan doesn't mean I'm getting married.'"

Suham was not surprised, since Michael had, that day when he'd eaten fried meat and tomatoes at her house, shocked her already. Now she worried he would neatly pack this sort of behavior into his luggage and take it overseas with him.

She had to find a solution. Just as she'd arranged their acquaintance, so must she assure their marriage.

"He says, `I'm going to Jordan on vacation," Wadi cried. "If I like the girl, I'll think about it.'"

"Oh *oughti, azzizti*, is this how you'll act in Jordan?"

Wadi moved slowly to the bed and sat down, heavy as a pregnant woman. She looked at the handkerchief in her hand, straightened it out, pressed hard on the creases and folded it neatly. Suham moved her sister's hair away from her eyes and watched her sad face.

"Is Aunt Wadi alright?" Nisreen asked, standing by the door and peeking into the bedroom like she used to do as a child.

"Go call Michael," Suham ordered.

Nisreen left at once and her footsteps were heard going down the stairs.

"Don't worry," Suham said. "I'll take care of this."

The two women said nothing to each other afterwards. It would be useless to speak of what a terrible son Michael was. Insults thrown at his face were of no use. How could they be of any use behind his back?

The room began to feel like a kitchen, as Wadi's tears salted the bed sheets and Suham's temper boiled the pillow feathers. Suham had had enough of

Michael's play. He must begin to take matters more seriously, or else her sister really would fall ill, God forbid.

First Michael's shadow appeared, and it took a long time before he presented himself. At least he had an ounce of shame, Suham thought, hoping his slowness meant he wouldn't come forth with a grin. With Michael one could never tell. Sometimes his behavior was as harmless as bread.

He stood against the door, staring at his aunt. Then he looked down to the floor, and just as he was about to let go of his seriousness, Suham warned, "Don't!"

The smile that nearly ripened was instantly wiped off his face. She didn't say a word, and to make him feel more uncomfortable, she didn't take her eyes off him, since in his case, one severe stare was never sufficient enough.

"Me and Rita think alike..." he began.

"Enough of that, please. Your mother already filled me in on your beautiful ideas."

He lowered his head again.

"You are not playing fair, and you can do that –" Suham glanced at Wadi. "But not without a price, Michael."

Wadi spilled more tears over the bed sheets as she re-examined her life with Michael out loud, going over the six days of this week, respectfully skipping the Sabbath.

"I have decided," Suham said. "Wadi will stay here in America."

Wadi's documentary paused in the middle of scene four.

"I'm going with you instead."

The room was as silent as Baghdad's streets during July afternoons, when the heat was so unbearable people stayed inside their homes and took naps under their ceiling fans.

He laughed spitefully at them both as his face changed, from a Chaldean to a werewolf. "It doesn't matter who comes with me," he growled. "But understand this, no one will be telling me what to do there!"

Suham was startled by his cruelty. She could imagine him tearing her and Wadi's flesh with his teeth if she didn't play dead.

Before dashing out the door, Michael banged the wall with his fist. Suham glanced at Wadi, Wadi glanced at Suham. She wanted to ask Wadi whether she could describe the beast they'd just encountered, in case the police asked. But Wadi had probably seen Michael's night mask before today, and was as accustomed to its black wrath as she was to her morning tea.

Suham realized she'd need God's help to undo whatever was done to Michael. But she wondered how that would be possible. She hadn't gone to church since Christmas and before that, since Easter; she prayed very little and she always tried to throw Wadi's Virgin Mary and Jesus pictures away. But God couldn't be shallow enough to hold these things against her.

She sighed, heavily. Like a pregnancy, the wedding had turned into a burden.

George turned into their street and passed the orange house. All its lights were off, and the lady of the house was sleeping beside her husband, beneath bed sheets that smelt of a woman's fragrance and covers that were as thick as women's thigh and just as soft. Her husband would get a kiss in the morning and better treats at night. She didn't have nephews and nieces to marry off, or sisters and brothers to support, because they all lived in different states.

Suham wondered if having two people to love was easier than having a dozen. In Baghdad it worked with food, where the variety was limited to fruits, vegetables, milk, cheese, bread, beef and chicken. In America, the fat-free butter, the no-yolk packaged eggs, the vegetarian sausages, and the frozen dinners threw one's appetite off.

"I have something to tell you, George," Suham gathered enough courage to say. "But I don't feel well enough to say it."

"About what?" he asked, concentrating too much on parking to pay attention to her.

She didn't answer, deciding to wait until he was less distracted.

"What's wrong?" he asked, watching her.

She turned towards him in a daze. The car door was open and half his body was outside.

"Nothing." She stepped out of the car.

Their footsteps echoed as if they were walking in a cave instead of their driveway. Inside, the house smelt of *iroog*, even though she had deep-fried the mixture of dough, parsley, cauliflower and onion patties in the garage early this morning for breakfast. She opened the glass door, and George complained the house would turn too cold.

"I want the smell of *iroog* to go away."

He turned his head left and right, and up and down as if his eyes would pick up the smell. "I don't smell anything."

Well, maybe you should try using your nose, she wanted to say, but didn't. "Come sit with me on the couch."

He frowned. "Now? With the door open?"

It seemed that every conversation she laid hand

on tonight was made complicated by the other party. That was fine with her, because most of her talents shone during trying times. "Suit yourself," she said and started walking up the stairs. "I have to do something, George, as much as I don't want to," she announced, as easily as she pealed tangerines. "And I think – actually I know – you won't like it."

He followed her up the stairs. "That means I won't be in it."

She smiled as she took off her earrings and bracelet and held them in her hands as delicately as she used to hold the raspberries she'd picked from her neighbor's house when she was a little girl in Baghdad. "You do impress me at times, *habbibi*, really."

"If I do, it's obviously not enough."

She entered her room, switched on the light, and prepared for her presentation, first placing her jewelry on the dresser to ascertain their safety, and then glancing at the mirror to be sure she looked pretty when she spoke.

When all was well, she turned around to face George. Sighing deeply, she leaned against the dresser and touched the back of her neck.

"Oh, I wish you understood," she said, her words pouring out of her lips as beautifully as fragrance poured out of jasmine. "You just don't know what I have to go through night and day."

He bent his eyes.

"Sometimes I wish I could be one of those ladies who walks around the house with a big grin on her face just because her husband desired her the night before," she said, maintaining the same grace she'd delivered a minute ago. "But I'm not that simple. And I don't know whether to consider myself fortunate or not in that way."

She didn't want to be more dramatic than that

and lose him altogether. Her head fell to the side, and like her husband, she stared at the beige carpet. She cleared her throat as he continued to listen. "Michael made Wadi cry today."

He met her eyes sympathetically before looking back down. She wondered if he thought she was giving a confession, and planned to remain quiet until she was done, when he'd tell her to say ten Hail Mary's and twenty Our Father's.

He was as terrible at catching hints as he was at gaining weight. "Wadi cannot go to Jordan with Michael," she cried. "George, it's impossible."

His eyes sprang up to her face. The mission was accomplished. He understood.

"This is a duty –"

He said nothing. There was yet another mission now, stroking his hurt feelings.

"I am your wife, yes, but God means for me to serve other people too – just like He has you serving the store."

His adam's apple bulged and his jaw tightened.

"I'm just going to marry him off. I'll be back in no more than three weeks –"

He ignored her by turning his face away.

"For God's sake, I went to Baghdad alone!"

He stared at the ceiling in exasperation.

"At least now there's a stronger reason."

He remained silent, and that made her doubt herself, her intentions, her decisions, everything. She crossed her arms beneath her breasts and sighed. The two of them were making great melodies with their huffs and hums.

"It's so hard to get a word out of you."

"My word has no value," he said and before she could plea for forgiveness, he disappeared into the bathroom.

Well, better for her. Let him make her hate him now, so when she left, she'd feel no guilt or regret. As she took off her dress, she listened to the water faucet running. She put on her nightgown and slipped inside the covers. George came out of the bathroom and without looking at her, got into bed.

"Aren't you going to speak to me?" she asked, unable to let him sleep with as much pain in his heart as there was lamb in his stomach.

He said nothing and rested his head on the pillow.

"Please, George…"

He snuggled so close to the covers, he smothered them.

"George, I want to talk to you –"

He surprised her by yanking the covers off of his body, the way she did the wax off her legs. Like a ball, he bounced out of bed, and with one quick motion, he snatched his pillow.

"George, don't be silly," she said as he sprinted to the door.

Gracefully, she remained sitting up on the bed, in case he returned. But forty minutes later, she huddled under the bed covers more so than George had, until she fell asleep.

Chapter 10

🙦

Suham sat on the patio the next morning, drinking coffee and smoking a cigarette. It felt like November, but today, unlike any other day, she loved the cold, because she realized it had the talent of absorbing stress as well as a menstrual cycle did. Winter days in Baghdad were as brief as the summer days in Michigan, so back then she didn't mind them. There, frost was as rare to see as bananas were to eat, as dear and expensive to Iraqis as lobster was to Americans. As a little girl walking to school, Suham would touch the cold white powder on the grass and lick it from her finger, thinking its taste would help explain her fascination with it.

Staring sadly into her own heart, Suham wished she could laminate Baghdad's memories so they'd never scratch or fade. They were her life. Where some people were killed by knives and bullets, Suham would die from the loss of her memory.

She heard the car engine start from the other end of the house. The sound of it stung her heart. The car backed out of the driveway and took off with full force. It was always with force that her husband wanted to get her attention, she smiled sadly.

Her eyes shifted to the sky. A flock of birds

danced in sync, like Chaldeans did in weddings during their ancient choreographed dance, the *depka,* where they held hands, made long lines which were headed by the people closest to the bride and groom, and all together did the same steps. It would be all worth it, she thought, and smiled.

Suham rushed to the travel agency to change Wadi's plane ticket to her name. The woman behind the desk glanced at the ticket for a moment then began typing top-secret things in the computer. "Okay, TWA to New York, leaving Detroit at five-fifteen… You will stay at Kennedy airport for six hours before your flight to Amman leaves."

The travel agent spoke casually, as if she was giving Suham a recipe and not an adventure. "What if I wanted to stay longer than a month?" she asked.

"There will be a hundred dollar charge."

The second she was handed the ticket Suham's mission became clearer than water and tastier than *pacha.* She couldn't remain still, though. She wanted to be shaken like dice in a gambler's hand or stirred like chickpeas in *tashreeb.*

Suham then made a stop at the supermarket, where she bought more canned soups and frozen dinners than when she had last traveled to Baghdad, since then, Nisreen was still living at home and was old enough to cook. And before the *asrunia,* the tea party Wadi planned on having for the ladies that evening as a farewell for Suham, the two sisters shopped at Kmart for gifts and trial-size bathroom items.

The ten-cent earrings on the blue-light special rack had Wadi in a frenzy. She insisted that Suham buy them all. "You never know who you'll run into over there."

Wadi talked of Jordan as though it was a small

village and not a country. But she was right. When one found one Chaldean he knew, one found a dozen – at least. Suham poured the fifty-some earrings into the shopping cart like sugar going into a coffee cup. The cart jingled as they went to the cosmetics aisle.

Wadi told Suham to pack the promotional KOOL T-shirts George had gotten from the cigarette company. "Give it to whoever is poor or helpful. It'll make them happy."

Suham bought two bottles of cologne for her cousin Saad, who planned on picking them up from the airport. Wadi told her that Saad's brother had a package of gifts, a letter, pictures and two hundred dollars to send with her.

While they were picking out a sweater for Saad, Wadi taught Suham, of all people, how by being a little more tactful, she could better manage Michael's mood swings. Then she snuck in a few hints about George's mutilated emotions and advised Suham to be a little more thoughtful.

"Please Wadi stop," Suham interrupted. "Just because I'm not satisfied with having food, clothes and a house doesn't make me a terrible person."

She threw the sweater into the shopping cart and headed towards the other end of the store.

"I have to restrain all my feelings for George, so he doesn't get upset, so he doesn't get hurt, so he doesn't hate. Yes, he's a good man, but that doesn't seem to make me any happier."

Wadi followed her down the toothpaste aisle. "I always knew you needed a man who'd break your neck."

Suham rolled her eyes, and quickened her pace. Maybe this vacation was more of a break from Wadi than it was from George. Wadi came after her as she'd had with Michael's blonde girl.

"Good men always get the onion peals, never the..."

Suham reined her vehicle and nearly dented the cereal display. She jumped off her fiery steed, pushed her cape back and looked sternly into Wadi's eyes. "If I'm strong enough not to complain about what George does to me, don't take advantage of it!"

Because they were pressed for time, what with Wadi having people over to send their relatives gifts with Michael, and Suham having to have to start packing, the *asrunia* was made simple with sesame cream, spinach and meat pies, sliced curd cheese with tomatoes, cucumber, parsley, olives, butter and marmalade, seeds and *dibess*, a syrup extracted from carob pods.

Wadi was upset that Suham, after having set the table, hadn't brought out the baklava, and she complained three times about it.

"Nobody wants baklava," Suham said, waving a fly away from the table. "Every time I take it out of the freezer and microwave it, it just sits in the middle of the table like flowers."

It was true. Because Chaldeans exchanged baklava like kisses, everyone was sick of it. A tray of baklava was bought to congratulate someone on a new home, or a newborn baby; it was given as a gift to those recently out of the hospital or who just arrived from a foreign country.

But whoever received the dessert did not welcome it, and since they couldn't give it back to its rightful owner, they usually gave it away to the next person who moved into a new house or had a baby, and so on and so forth.

On many less fortunate occasions, the house that originally received the tray of baklava got stuck with it. For some odd reason, it never dawned upon anyone to buy a different gift and save the hostess or the patient the trouble of finding freezer space for this dessert.

"There's only cardamom seeds in here." Wadi nearly dipped her nose into the cup of tea. "I forgot the mint."

"I'll go pick some," Leka said.

"Don't worry about cardamom," Alia sang, "don't worry about mint, don't worry, my sister, about anything but a man's ding-a-lings."

"What kind of nonsense you talk," Wadi said, but she couldn't resist smiling.

Alia threw watermelon seeds into her mouth without pealing them first. She had the manners of a drunkard. "Why shouldn't I talk nonsense – I'm not a scientist."

Suham grinned. "Oh, aren't you?"

Alia frowned, but as she was about to say something, the sight of Leka interrupted her. Pressing peppermint leaves tightly against her bosom, like the old ladies did their rosaries in church, she nervously asked Suham if she could fit a pair of shoes and a white baptism dress inside her luggage.

Alia said those things sounded heavy, yet fragile, the worst type. Her stuff, though, was simpler; a family size-pack of Tylenol, a bottle of Clinique moisturizer, and a few Wet & Wild lipsticks. Sabria said she had heavy, but not fragile items, four cans of peanut butter and a jacket.

Suham agreed to take their things, and the ladies rushed to the car to bring out their bags. Everything was reasonable except for the cans of peanut butter, which were each the size of dictionaries.

"You know, I'm not going to Baghdad myself," Suham said. "I'm sending these things with Rita's mother."

Sabria explained how her friend was on the WIC program and since she received peanut butter once a month, her closet was stacked with it. So she handed them to friends and family. It would be a shame, she told Suham, to let them go to waste, especially when they were going to Iraqis, who found any excuse to fast from meat.

After much time and effort, the ladies talked Sabria out of sending two of the cans. Suham would've pushed for leaving out one more can, but Sabria, being her oldest brother's wife, had to be given extra respect. So Suham twisted her tongue, tied its ends together and made it into an ankle bracelet.

The ladies then sent one of the little girls to bring down a large yellow envelope sitting on top of the refrigerator. When it arrived, Wadi withdrew Rita's picture from the envelope more carefully than she would an x-ray, and like a deck of cards, the 8x10 portfolio went from hand to hand around the table. The compliments about her hair and skin and legs and arms, already once discussed and dissected, were repeated just as enthusiastically now as they had been the first time.

Finally, the ladies left the picture on the table, gathered up their children, and went home. By doing the dishes and chatting with some of Wadi's later guests, Suham postponed going home. Now that the ticket was bought, it was harder to face George.

When she got home, though, facing George wasn't the problem she'd anticipated. Finding him was. She knew he wouldn't be at his mother's, because he loved her too much to humiliate her. He wouldn't be in a bar – he didn't go to them before he got married, how would he know where they were now? The farthest he'd be was at Denny's, and the most harmful thing he'd be doing was drinking coffee and having cherry cheesecake.

She stayed up until she heard keys rattling and the door opening. She dove inside the covers, in case he wanted to change into his pajamas yet didn't want to associate with her. But she left the lights on, in case her hair, neck and shoulders could bait him. He never made it upstairs, though. So she threw away her alluring posture and dunked completely into the covers.

Wadi came to Suham's house the next day, to help her prepare for the trip. The ladies turned the house into an Olympic stadium with the way they sped up and down the stairs and ran in and out of the rooms. Suham made Nisreen a list of errands that covered things like taking Wadi to the market and doing George's laundry; cooking his meals four days a week, since Wadi offered to do it the other three days, except for the days George went to his mother's; and visiting her aunt and her father at least five times a week, to see what they needed. The garbage got picked up on Thursday. Never use the back door so she'd avoid forgetting it unlocked. The car must stay in the garage, and spoiled food must be tossed in the trash.

Suham's son, Rafid, came to spend the weekend after being informed she was leaving for a month. The first thing she did with him was lead him into the kitchen and ask him what he wanted to eat.

"How about some *chilli-fry*?" he asked, making her shudder.

Chilli-fry wasn't the most complicated Arabic cuisine, but it dealt with chopping lots of onions and tomatoes, defrosting lots of meat and cutting it into small cubed pieces; then in the right order – onion, meat, tomatoes – allowing the ingredients to lazily sizzle in the skillet.

Since Suham, of course, wouldn't dream of denying her son a wish, she started in on it right away. She was chopping the onions when she spotted Wadi marching towards her like the football players on TV, reminding her so much of her mother. Wadi grabbed the knife from her hands and told her to go away.

Suham moved to the side and watched her sister's creation. The onions were chopped too thin, so their flavor would be lost. She wanted to correct her, but realized that for weeks Wadi would be fixing George's food without supervision anyway. She went upstairs to pack.

Halfway through her work, she took a break and went downstairs again. Rafid had already eaten dinner and was now watching a show about jets or pilots – she couldn't tell which – on the History Channel, while Wadi stood over the sink, washing dishes.

She told Wadi to leave the dishes alone and Wadi said to go away, and she did go, to where her son was sitting.

"Don't buy any red hats with tassels," he warned.

She smiled and kissed his forehead. "You tell me what you want, *iyouni*, and I'll get it for you."

He thought about it. "Those things with long pipes that men smoke."

"Ah, a *nerghile*."

He nodded his head, smiling. "Yes, yes."

She marveled at his features, like he was an infant who had just been placed in her arms by a nurse. "I hope you know that when you're done with college, the only landlord you'll have is your dad and me."

"I know."

As if she'd come simply to throw that at him,

she stood up to leave. "I'm going out with your dad tonight, so can you drop your aunt off at home?"

"Yeah."

Holding his face in her hands, she kissed his forehead. She pulled away and observed him one last time, like a little girl did her doll before leaving her on the dresser and going to sleep. She went back upstairs with Wadi to continue her packing.

George agreed to dine out more easily than Suham had expected. He must want her to pluck the thorns off his heart, as if he had one or two, not a truckload. Besides, she didn't have the right tools to heal him. She only had two hands and half-a-heart.

Contrary to George's better expectations, they were already arguing by the time they were two blocks away from their house. He said Wadi and Michael weren't children and that she should let them run their own lives. She said he was jealous of her family. One word from him, three words from her, and she erupted, "Take me home!"

He swerved the car into an empty lot, backed up, swung around, and made a left turn, his tires squealing. He must be having the time of his life, Suham thought. She would have said something to stop his silliness, but she didn't want to be the boxer fighting the referee in the ring.

Then he started in on other stunts, like hitting red lights and slamming hard on the brakes before making a turn. She squeezed the door handle with each incident and rolled her eyes to every jolt. It took as much effort to keep quiet as it did for him to talk.

But if she didn't say something, his ridiculous behavior would not stop. The last thing she wanted, with her trip the day after tomorrow, was an accident or a ticket. Or both. So she begged him to turn into a parking lot.

Having been tossed like a salad, she asked him to give her a minute to collect her thoughts. He waited as she calmed herself. She turned to him and placed her hand on his face.

"Is it easier to drive like that than it is to tell me how you feel?"

Tightening his jaw, he looked straight ahead. "I don't want you to go."

She lifted the armrest between them and slid over. "You shouldn't always consider my feelings first."

"This is how I love you," he said. "I can't change that."

She leaned her head on his shoulders.

"Why do you get so busy doing stuff like this?"

"Because if I left it to anyone else, it wouldn't be done." She raised her head, turned his chin towards her and looked into his eyes. "Is it wrong to do good for the family?"

He leaned a little towards the steering wheel, started the car, drove home and made love to her. She was happy. She'd plucked the thorns out of his heart.

Chapter 11

The plane ride cradled Suham's spirit and helped put her to sleep, like soup easily could. Sitting in a crowd felt as peaceful as standing in front of a waterfall. The environment, run by the stewardesses as orderly as cattle were by shepherds, reminded her of Baghdad, a city where people of different class and religion worked as passionately together as *mesaki'a*, the dish of assorted vegetables which, although they were fried separately, met in the same casserole, led first by chunks of cooked meat on the bottom, then covered by a layer of onion rings, then a layer of green pepper loops, then round potato slices, then oval eggplant wedges, and last, a layer of tomato circles. It was as colorful a dish as a five-topping pizza.

Amman's airport felt hot and sticky. It looked like the stock market of the Middle East, with men everywhere, dressed in as many garments as they would've worn for a wedding and instructing each other with strong voices and impatient eyes.

Saad awaited their arrival, pushed against the pick-up parcel's window to salute their Made-in-China gifts of perfume, jewelry, belts and wool sweaters. His moustache and beard disguised him pretty well, but Suham still spotted him quickly.

Saad greeted Michael and Suham with fireworks
and cannons, and a bouquet of flowers for the lovely
lady. Suham thought the flowers were as overdone as
taking two trays of baklava into a new home, but she
looked at the bright side. At least they weren't roses,
which would've made her feel uncomfortable. Suham
accepted the flowers with a half-hearted smile and a
quiet "thank you". Then she placed a "beware" sign
between her breasts and thighs.

Saad hugged and kissed Michael while eagerly
telling him what an honor it was to have him, and his
aunt, as his guests. The big hand on Suham's watch
moved two notches before her turn came up. Saad
shook her hands in a business-like manner and he
kissed her on each cheek, with only his clean-shaved
skin, and not his lips, touching. His behavior was
quite appropriate, although it caused Suham to smile
devilishly, knowing how for him, standing in front of
her must have been as difficult to do as standing in
font of Saddam would've been.

The last time she'd seen Saad was on her wedding
day. He'd sat in a corner, drunk beer, and left early.
A few weeks earlier, when he'd heard that a man from
America had come to ask for Suham's hand, he'd
taken on the role of Romeo, and failed. He'd thrown
words about how much he loved Suham to people as
carelessly as a woman threw a bucket of dirty water
in the streets after she finished mopping her kitchen
floor. He took this course of wooing her, since Suham
had made it difficult for him to confront her face to
face, to deliver the message to her ears. His hopes
that it would touch her heart and stop her from marrying the man from America had never had a chance.

Suham was flattered that the entire Chaldean
community knew how much Saad loved her, but that
was about all she felt when she heard the news. For

years, she'd been as aware of his love as she was of her beauty. And for this reason, she'd avoided him, fearing that he'd one day build up enough courage to say "I love you" and in return, she'd burst into laughter.

Suham revealed to a cousin why she couldn't marry Saad. "He's an ordinary boy who still plays with marbles on his father's porch."

"Today he's a boy, tomorrow he'll be a man."

"Well, I'm thinking about today before tomorrow," Suham had said. "Besides, I want to go to America."

The cousin said she didn't blame her, since there, she'd be having maids, cooks and gardeners.

Saad married many years later, but his wife was said to have been so wicked, just her stare alone could kill a hen, and that within a year, she, along with the military, had managed to scare him away. So he'd fled to Jordan.

Suham's eyes, ears and nose captured the Arabic words, the dry smells and the loud honks around her, and she stored them in her heart. She'd smuggle them over the border, to the United States, and have her way with them on her patio.

"This place is a chaos, you have to admit," Michael said.

Suham rolled her eyes and shook her head.

"Look at those guys over there." Michael pointed to the left, where a short bald man, a tall skinny man and a fat man huddled around each other near their taxicabs. They were smoking and spitting on the sidewalk. They were talking to prospective passengers too, one of them being Saad.

"You know what those are?" He laughed hysterically before delivering the punch line.

Her eyes warned him not to start, but he did

anyway.

"Those are MacDaddy #1, MacDaddy #2 and MacDaddy #3."

She sighed, heavily.

He turned his head left and right and seemed annoyed. "There are barely any women here. How am I supposed to find a wife, damn it?"

"The same way you found the travel agent," she said, sarcastically.

He smiled.

"And one more thing," she said. "Don't call the people of this country DaddyMacs, or what have you."

He laughed so hard his face turned as red as her lipstick. Realizing she'd said the word wrong, but not knowing how, she cracked a smile. "Your mother did a good thing by staying home."

"Didn't she though?"

"You don't know how happy it makes me to be in your presence," Saad said in the most formal fashion, while sitting in the passenger seat of the taxi.

Michael arched his brows. "Even though we didn't exactly come here to visit you, but to marry me?"

"Don't pay attention to him, Saad," Suham said. "Or else he'll have you believe there are no palm trees in Baghdad, but there are Bedouins in Michigan."

"Is that right, Michael?"

"Yeah."

Saad laughed. "Don't worry, God loves humor."

Her body lightly rocking in the taxi, Suham looked at Michael with compassionate eyes. "I hope so."

The taxi drove them to the Hilton. The hotel room had two twin size beds, a television set, striped drapery and a framed picture of Petra on the wall. Suham gathered the drapery to one side and opened the window. The city of Amman faced her, bright because of the sun, but quiet out of habit, unlike her friend, Baghdad.

She sighed. Only fifteen hours away, yet she couldn't say hello to her beloved city in person.

The men set the luggage on the floor, and Michael suggested they visit Rita.

"But they're expecting us tomorrow," Suham said.

"She knows we're arriving today. She probably hopes we'll see her right away so the suspense wouldn't kill her."

Suham considered it. Rita didn't have a phone, and she didn't want to catch her off guard. Yet she was just as impatient to see her as Michael was. "Maybe she's not prepared."

"Let's discover her natural beauty then." He turned to Saad and smiling, he patted his shoulder. "What do you say?"

"*Wallah*, I don't know. Your aunt has to make the call here."

They both looked at her and awaited a reply. Suham gave her permission and they prepared to leave the hotel. Suham brushed her hair, Michael combed his. She dampened her face with a towel, he splashed his with water. She grabbed her purse and headed toward the door, but he wouldn't stop staring at himself in the mirror. Suham tried to rush him, complaining it was getting late and she was getting tired.

He turned to her and posed. "Does my hair look okay?"

His soft eyes were like a switch that turned off her impatience. He reminded her of a baby, despite his height, weight and his stubbles. "You look fine."

"Okay. Lets go!"

It was nighttime, and the air outside felt cooler. Taxis were lined up near the hotel's main entrance and Saad waived for one. Hardly any guests walked in or out of the hotel. By the end of spring, Suham told Michael, expect to see blond hair, blue-eyed tourists.

"Why in the world would Europeans come to visit Jordan?" Michael asked her.

"For Petra or the Dead Sea."

"Who wants a dead sea? People can go to Cancun and see the best ocean on earth."

"Where's Cancun?" Saad asked.

"It's in Mexico," Michael said, excited. "They have these great restaurants – I mean, you go to Planet Hollywood and see TV screens the size of this hotel. And Mr. Pappas – girls dancing on the bar table while you're eating your steak!"

Saad seemed a bit embarrassed by Michael's bluntness, but he laughed. He must be as charmed by Michael as everyone else was. "The Dead Sea is so salty," Saad said, "you can't swim in it – you just float."

Michael shook his head and squinted his eye as if he'd just eaten a lemon. "The Dead Sea – no American would want to come here for a vacation. No way!"

"Michael, easy *habbibi*," Suham said. "We're not talking about the war here."

The drive to Rita's house was pleasant, because while the men dissected politics, Suham rolled down the window and observed the city. Not too many people were out, but watermelon booths were lined up less than 100 yards from each other. There was a lot of construction machinery on enormous empty land, the way there was on M-59, a route she took to get to Lakeside Mall.

Suham had lived in Amman for a few months after she'd married because her immigration papers couldn't be processed in Baghdad. Back then the citizens of Amman became as quiet at night as a disco did in the morning. It was different now, not lively, especially not by an Iraqi's standard, but different. It could be that God was impregnating Jordanians with passion, the way He'd impregnated Iraqis with patience.

The taxi parked beside a curb, across from a chicken booth, and the driver asked some boys for directions. While some talked over each other to the driver, others peeked inside while others yet kept their hands in their pockets and their eyes to the ground. Even though they didn't know where the address was, they continued to loiter around the cab. The taxi driver cussed beneath his breath and took off before they wasted any more of his time.

He stopped again at a gas station, and before the car braked, Saad flung open its door and sped towards a man to ask for directions.

"Why is he doing that and not you?" Michael asked the driver.

The driver shook his head, looking at Saad with much the same amazement as he would at a talking tree. "So he'd come back and explain to me what that man explained to him, and what he himself couldn't understand."

Michael laughed, and Suham smiled. It was amusing how Saad tried to impress them, who were fresh from the land of Rocky, Rambo and Jurassic Park. The poor man didn't know that what impressed Michael was his own charm. What impressed Suham was the feminine art.

Suham asked Michael what was taking Saad long.

"Confusion," Michael said.

Saad returned to the car just before the driver was going to go down and fetch him by the ear. He took a deep breath before untangling the mystery; he told them that Rita's address was in so and so street, near so and so building. They drove on, ending up in a busy neighborhood.

Some old men sat on the apartment building's doorsteps, while others sat on chairs, beads in their hands and wisdom in their eyes. There were children sitting with them and riding bikes. A bunch of younger men smoked cigarettes and stood beside a booth selling roasted chicken that neighbored the apartment building.

"There it is," the driver said.

The men fought amongst themselves to pay the driver, but Saad won, not that he had a choice really. To have allowed Michael to pay, when they only arrived in Jordan that day, would be as inhospitable as allowing a sister who'd come from out of town to stay in a hotel. Although Michael, to whom tradition in its littlest forms seemed as foreign as Portuguese, might not have seen it that way.

They got out of the taxi, and the smell of dust, cooking chicken and human sweat rushed over them, like a red carpet for royalty. Her majesty straightened her blouse and curled her hair behind her ear, while his majesty pulled up his jeans and adjusted his belt. Saad observed the building, in case it was wired.

With eyes turned on them from every corner of the neighborhood, they paraded towards the building. The chicken fumes clung to Suham's hair and clothes, and she yearned for a *shawarma* sandwich with beets, tomatoes, cucumbers, and yogurt sauce.

Keeping in mind that she was being watched as closely as the Queen of England, she lifted her skirt an inch or so from the ground, held her chin up high, maintained a serious expression, moved swiftly, and never made eye contact with any of the men.

Inside, the building spooked her. It was as hollow as the chocolate Easter bunny George ordered for his store every year, and there was every smell imaginable. Suham didn't need to wonder about what the lady behind the closed doors cooked for supper, as she had with the orange house back home.

Here she had a pretty good idea how an Arabic lady cooked. She stirred tomato paste with simmering onions and chunks of meat, then added okra or eggplants, or whatever other vegetable she had in her refrigerator and her husband happened to crave; she scrubbed pots and pans as hard as she would the red wine spilled on her white dress; she spoke harshly with her children and softer with her husband. Since society molded a man's heart into metal, the women needed more heat to reach him than she did to cook *mambari*, stuffed sheep's intestines.

"Hold onto me," Saad said to Michael, leading them along. She was reminded of the time she'd gone grape leaf picking with Wadi, in a field as dark as eggplants and as empty as the inside of a green pepper.

"Hold onto me," Michael said to Suham, while he put his hand on Saad's shoulder. Michael didn't have Rita's apartment number, not that there were numbers on the door. But he knew it was on the third floor, so they climbed the stairs.

The silence of the place, the echoing of their footsteps, and the heaviness of the dark felt as adventurous as walking in Baghdad's *souk*, between distinguished merchants, rainbow colored fabrics, and exciting spicy smells.

On the third floor, there were three doors to choose from, and as though they'd lose a prize if they

knocked on the wrong one, they waited, hoping someone would come along to direct them. There was no
one though.

"Maybe they're all stranded outside," Michael
said.

Saad laughed, then Michael laughed, and the
building shook. So the ceiling wouldn't start spilling
plaster over their heads, Suham sacrificed her laughter by clenching her teeth and tensing her neck.

"Stop it, Michael, they might hear us," Suham
said, when she saw that Michael's sarcasm was soaking Saad for too long.

Although she'd made the comment to Michael,
Saad was the one who obeyed. Michael, on the other
hand, scoffed at the situation without mercy. Suham
called upon his name a dozen times, but his infatua-
tion with his own jokes had swallowed him whole. He
couldn't hear a word.

"What am I going to do with him?" Suham asked
Saad.

A rock must have hit Michael's stomach, because
his cynical world-view died instantly. He changed
from a jack-in-the-box to a legislator, and he pointed
to the left door beside him. "I think it's this one."

"I think it's this one," Saad suggested, his hands
pointing towards the right door.

Suham rewarded Saad a look of approval, since
she didn't trust Michael would knock, rather than
beat out music, on the door. Saad took a deep breath,
pulled his sleeves up, and knocked three times.
Then, out of consideration for the occupants of the
apartment, he moved to the side and allowed Suham
to stand in front of him; whoever would open the door
would not be as frightened to see a strange woman as
they would a strange man.

Chapter 12

❧

he lady who opened the door was in her late thirties. Because she was tall and light-colored, she did not look Arabic. If she decided to smuggle into America with a fake passport, it wouldn't be a problem. She could easily pass for German or French, Danish or English. The only thing she'd need to worry about were the officials who'd stop her to note the beauty she was importing.

She greeted them like she would her lifelong friends, smiling at them in different scales and helloing them in more than one word. This must be the right apartment, Suham thought.

"Does a girl by the name of Rita reside here?"

"She does," the lady answered. "I'm her cousin, Hannan. Please, won't you come in?"

Suham tiptoed through the hallway, giving Rita a chance to take the cucumber slices off her eyes and the curlers out of her hair. As she turned into the family room, she caught a glimpse of *al qamar* sitting on the couch, near the television set.

The last time Suham had seen such a bright moon was years ago, when George had gone down to the kitchen to eat her leftover cucumber stew. She'd told him she'd stay in bed, but she'd changed her mind within a minute and headed downstairs. She remembered him standing over the pot of cold stew, tagging the cucumber and meat inside it with a spoon.

"Why don't you heat it up?" she'd asked.

He looked up at her in confusion. Then when he seemed to have grasped what she'd said, he glanced at the pot and considered. Smiling, she walked towards him and slid the pot from beneath his nose. She'd taken such special care of his food that night that she did not microwave it, but instead poured a portion of it into a smaller pot and warmed it over fire.

She'd watched him the first few minutes as he ate, but then she'd reached her hands and softly stroked his face. The rate at which he'd been chewing slowed down like the pulse of a runner at rest.

"Eat, *habbibi*," she'd said and she left the table. She went to the kitchen and made cardamom tea while he finished his food. They'd drunk the tea on the patio, she sitting across from him, with her cup in her lap and her feet in his lap. They watched a "father moon" – that was what Suham called it, since it was twice its normal size.

They'd talked about things from the Far East, like the deer and hunters, Cleopatra and her lovers, the cows and their worshipers. When she'd fallen silent, he'd kissed her knees and asked to hear more of her voice, and when he'd stopped drawing lines across her feet, she'd asked to feel more of his touch. It was one of the nicest nights, because if a chemist could have measured the energy of love given and taken from each side, he would come out with equal figures.

Rita's smile was as sweet as white apricots and her eyes were as tender, as tasty even as pastries. The rivers of Baghdad themselves couldn't have been any prettier than she. She had her arms locked around a child who leaned against her legs, whom she'd either positioned to show her motherly nature or to occupy herself until the guests finished inspecting her. Whichever the case might have been, it gave a superb impression. A frustrated man would start looking into himself once he'd see her, instead of being angry at why God had created the universe.

The company took their seats. In Arabic homes, introductions for the most part were left to the imagination. One either had to be clever enough to recognize the cabbage from the lettuce, or they had to be attentive enough to figure it out later in conversations. For instance, in this case, it was obvious that the old man was the uncle, the older lady the mother, the younger man was Hannan's husband, and the child their son.

Suham was secure in the fact that Saad wouldn't be mistaken for Michael and vice-versa. Aside from the clothes and hairstyle that set them apart, Michael looked as serene as a spiritual book. In Iraq, a suitor dressed in armor and, with a bag of twenty-four karat gold strapped around his stomach, rode a horse through a girl's home. Michael would've done that, perhaps, if he had been going to buy mischief from the bazaar.

Rita moved the child to the side, as gently as if she was removing a diamond bracelet from her wrists, and she stood up. Suham explored every detail, starting from the thick sandals on her feet and moving up towards the gold cross against her chest, as she went into another room with her cousin.

"How was your flight?" Najat, Rita's mother, inquired.

"It went as scheduled," Suham said.

"*Nishkur Allah*," Najat thanked God and then told the story of how their bus was delayed for eight hours because Customs were searching everyone hard, and some they'd searched twice.

"We had nine suitcases, filled with Rita's clothes, silk quilts and food spices. I wanted her to take them to America." Najat pinched her dress's fabric and lifted it an inch. "For her sake, I've come with only one dress on my back. And so what do they do at Customs? They flip Rita's clothes in the air like feathers and they scramble them like eggs."

She imitated the inspector's movements with her hands.

"They stood there, like rocks, and watched us struggle to fit the clothes back into the luggage. Then two nice officers had pity on us and came to help."

Shakir, Rita's uncle, shook his head while staring at the beads in his hand. "What a mess. What a mess." He lifted his eyes to Suham. "You probably don't get searched in America, do you?"

"We do, but we don't feel it." Like we don't feel our neighbor's hearts, or our husband's love, she said to herself.

Hannan appeared with a tray of sodas, and one by one she served the guests. Shortly afterwards Rita returned, her hands empty, and took her seat. Suham turned to ask Saad for the time and she noticed Michael's eyes fixed on Rita. He seemed fascinated and pleased about the merchandise, as they teased in Arabic.

Hannan handed her husband a note and then he departed. The two families returned to comparing American immigration officials to those of Iraq. Amongst the conversation, Rita told a story of having entrusted a man who was able to cross the Iraqi border without being searched to deliver a gold necklace, six bracelets and a ring to Jordan.

"Do you trust him?" Suham asked.

"Oh Abu-Ahmad!" she said. "He's an excellent man."

Najat said that they'd also entrusted money with this man and hoped he'd deliver the items safely. They were basically hinting that the gold, which was a portion of Rita's dowry, and the money, which would've covered some of their expenses, might be confiscated at the border by the inspection guards.

To Suham, this story sounded as fictional as Rambo. If she was to search Rita's bedroom in Baghdad right now, she'd probably find the gold laid out on the dresser, next to the jewelry box, awaiting Najat to give it as a gift for one of her son's brides when they married.

"He gave us a number where we could reach him," Rita said. "But they don't know his whereabouts either."

Whether they were lying or not, although most likely they were, didn't matter. It was common for a girl to smuggle as much fortune as she could into her mother's bosom before leaving her father's home. This scandal in itself didn't make Rita any less suitable a bride.

Dinner arrived from the restaurant in two large trays, one of shish kebab with whole grilled onions and tomatoes, the other of rotisserie chicken with roasted potatoes. On a separate small tray, there was hot bread from the oven, pickles and parsley.

Hannan's hospitality embarrassed Suham. Since her family were refugees, the last thing they could afford was costly dinners. But Suham relieved herself with the thought that, once Rita left her cousin's home to be financially embraced by her fiancé, Michael would make it up to them by inviting them to his place and introducing them to his aunt's hospitality.

So much politics was discussed during dinner,

Suham felt like she was watching CNN. But when they started drinking tea, she heard stories that made her feel she was inside the news room, reading a piece before it went into the editor's hands.

She heard how the Gulf War injured Iraq's wealth, but benefited Jordan's poverty, because the Iraqis who'd fled there had no jobs but kept money flowing. Refugees called their relatives in America once a month, described their harsh conditions, and asked for a *waraka* – paper in the Arabic vocabulary, a hundred-dollar bill in subtle hints.

Suham smiled. "Do they think a hundred-dollar bill is our hourly pay?"

Najat told her how she'd gotten nauseous yesterday when she'd read in the classified adds that the Jordanians were in need of maids. "They wanted Egyptians or Iraqi women!"

This news had such an impact on Suham she quivered. For her, it made more history than the war itself.

The dinner trays were carried away, and with them the gloomy facts about Iraq's condition. It was late when the tea was served, so they gulped it down like orange juice. There was a certain emptiness in the room, as though everyone wanted to hurry up and say good night. It was Suham's job to initiate their exit and when she got to her feet the rest jumped at the chance to escort her out the door, all the mean-while saying, "Won't you please stay longer?"

Suham thanked them for their hospitality and insisted that she and Michael return to their hotel. She'd had a long flight, she needed to change, she was sleepy, she knew they wanted her to leave.

"It has been an honor," Hannan said. Goodbye. Goodbye. Goodbye. Goodbye.

"Yes, it has really been an honor," Najat said.

Goodbye. Goodbye. Goodbye.

Rita's family, unable to shed a word about any arrangements concerning the courting process between Michael and Rita (that was the man's duty), prolonged their goodbyes. They'd probably hoped that if Michael wouldn't say anything, at least Suham would. But although his aunt, Suham was as much imprisoned by fear as they were. Hers, of course, was of a different nature. If she opened her mouth, Michael might have a public outburst and the establishment they'd just dined in would have the guards kick them into the streets.

"Why don't you and your daughter leave your cousin's house and stay with us at the hotel?" Michael suggested to Rita's mother.

Rita and her relations looked nearly ready to faint at this, after they'd worked so hard to sweep empty bottles and shattered glass out of Michael's way so he would reach this point. Suham wasn't any less relieved.

They left eight pieces of Rita's luggage behind, saying that they'd pick them up after they found an apartment, and left for the hotel.

The hotel looked nicer at night. Of course, it might have improved in Suham's eyes now that Michael was going through the first stages of love, when the man pursued a girl faster than he did a new job. For the lady, this was the most effortless stage, where she did nothing but think the world of herself.

The man behind the desk asked to see Rita's and Najat's passports. The two women searched their purses.

"I want both rooms in my name," Michael stressed to the man, for the second time.

"I understand sir," the man said in his professional manner. "But we still need to see their passports."

Rita found hers, but her mother didn't. She said it might be at Hannan's apartment or maybe in one of the suitcases. She couldn't recall. Michael tried convincing the receptionist to give them the additional room without the hassle, but the man held on tightly to the hotel's policy.

Suham waited patiently, praying they wouldn't have to drive back to Hannan's apartment and risk returning Rita to her family. She wanted the tracks that Michael was driving his train on to continue without interruption, so they wouldn't risk losing a cargo or two. The passport finally turned up between a folded towel in Najat's bigger bag. Once that was over, Saad wished the women and Michael a good night and excused himself.

"You want to have a drink at the bar?" Michael asked.

The women quickly glanced at each other. It was Suham's queue; she either encouraged the invitation or they didn't go. "Yes, why not?" Suham said.

The ladies followed Michael down some steps to a dark and quiet bar, with red empty chairs, soft jazz and thick cigarette smoke that hadn't exited the place with its smoker. The ladies ordered coffee, and Michael a beer.

While adding milk and sugar to her cup, Suham listened to the flow of Michael and Rita's talk. She kept her eyes to herself, and to give them additional privacy, she started a conversation with Rita's mother. From it, Suham learned that Najat had had three miscarriages, that her husband was a sergeant in the army with a medical degree, that Rita's three younger brothers didn't serve in the military because they were college students, and because they had connections with people who worked under Saddam.

Suham listened attentively to Najat, while the wind kept blowing Rita's giggles, the cigarette smoke, and Michael's smiling tone, towards her direction. And during pauses and breaks, her ears peeked into their room and she heard them making love.

"What is your natural hair color?" Suham asked, greatly affected by Rita's hair, which was as thick and smooth as old-fashioned curtains.

Rita touched a few strands and smiled shyly. "It's this."

"It looks as though it has been highlighted with henna."

Rita blushed. "That's what everyone says. But it's naturally *tamari*." The color of dates.

It was after one o'clock in the morning. The women had finished drinking their coffee and Michael his beer, and to have pushed the night any further wouldn't have held any purpose. Suham suggested they end the night. Everyone agreed.

Suham with Najat, while Michael walked with Rita, they escorted them to their room on the fourth floor. Even though they'd strolled down the hallway as slowly as horse carriage drove in the streets, Michael and Rita did not want to part from each other. They wanted another ride.

Seeing that this marriage wouldn't be as complicated as she'd anticipated, Suham wished they had gone with the original plan, of Wadi doing the honors of delivering her son to his fiancée. It didn't feel good to have taken such a privilege from her sister, but Suham had changed the arrangements with good intentions. She didn't know Michael would come to his senses faster than she chopped parsley.

"So what did you think, *habbibi*?" Suham asked

Michael in the room, although she knew the answer.

Michael's head on the pillow, he stared at the ceiling with awe. "She's beautiful."

"Can you see yourself with her?"

"Very much."

Suham wanted to record this conversation, the first serious one she'd had with Michael for years. "She's a very nice girl, don't you think?"

He pondered this question longer than she considered normal, and she held her breath, in case she'd be thrown into deep water. "Isn't she sort of short?"

Yes she was, Suham thought, though she hadn't imagined him to take such quick notice. She'd assumed that, given her outstanding traits, and because he was as taken by her as he was by the Red Wings, Michael would be as unaware of Rita's height as he was to the number of hooks on her brassiere.

"She's more petite than I remembered her to be," Suham said, a bit disappointed with her previous estimation. Rita had seemed much taller in Baghdad, although, now come to think of it, she'd never observed her standing up.

Over the phone, Rita had given Suham her measurements by the Arabic metric system, in inches. Suham then did her research, transferred the inches into feet, and came up with five feet, less one inch. "Who do we have that's five feet tall?" Suham had asked at the Easter dinner, and one of her nieces had raised her hand. They made the girl stand in the middle of their circle and had examined her from head to toe. In the end, they'd concluded that such height for a lady was decent, especially when Michael was no more than 5'6". No one had expected that an inch difference would turn an average height to that of below average.

"I was watching the two of you walk beside each

other," Suham said, when she saw he planned on remaining quiet. "You are compatible in size."

He didn't give a standing ovation, nor did he clap.

"She's a doll, *habbibi*."

"Yes, she's pretty," he said in a daze. "I mean maybe we shouldn't wait too long before we get married."

This boy was harder to understand than the Arab leaders. "It's up to you, darling, how long you want to wait." She'd strived not to show her excitement and in return, spoil his.

"She's prettier than the pictures."

"The pictures did her no justice."

"And her personality..."

"The phone didn't do her any more justice than the pictures had."

"Why wait, right?"

"Michael, *habbibi*, before you came here, your one fear was that you might not feel chemistry towards Rita. Now that that's out of the way – I'm assuming it is, anyway, from what I saw tonight – don't be so hesitant."

"What about her height?"

"She's my height," Suham lied.

"She's shorter. She's very short."

"Well, thank God it's her height and not her figure."

"Yeah," he sighed, still staring at the ceiling. "We'll tell them tomorrow that the wedding will be next Friday."

"*Allah kareem*," she said.

Suham was now glad Wadi hadn't come, because sometimes Michael behaved as strangely as a woman's hormones. And Wadi had a hard enough time dealing with her own medical problems to attend to Michael's.

Suham, on the other hand, hungrily awaited such patients, the way George awaited 24-case beer buyers.

Chapter 13

✤

Suham phoned Rita's room the next morning and asked her what time would be most convenient for her and her mother to meet at the restaurant downstairs. Rita said it didn't matter to them, and Suham said it didn't matter to them, either. They put each other's feelings too much into consideration before mutually agreeing upon eleven o'clock.

Suham shouted this message onto Michael through the bathroom door, and while waiting for him to get ready, she pulled open the curtains, sat on the bed and smoked a cigarette. But unlike in her family room, she couldn't sit still for as long as one cigarette, much less four or five. Here it was a shame to sit behind the window and not be a part of it.

At eleven-twenty, she knocked on the bathroom door as impatiently as she turned off a soap opera. "Come on, Michael. They're waiting for us."

The water faucet turned on and off three times while she paced in the room. She restrained herself from knocking some more and yelling at him, because she feared it'd only stoke his tardiness. At eleven-thirty, the curtains were drawn and Michael appeared on stage.

"Is my hair okay?" he asked.

Suham rolled her eyes, exasperated, and marched out of the hotel room. Rita and her mother were already sitting in the restaurant, on a Royal-shaped table that could fit eight people, Rita wearing jeans, her mother the same dress she had on yesterday. They had had their teas in front of them, had probably remarked on their friends' tardiness, and had considered ordering the eggs, but courteously didn't.

Suham apologized for being late, hoped they hadn't waited too long, complimented their sunny table, and took her seat next to Michael, across from the two ladies. She asked the waiter for a cup of tea, and then her attention was distracted by the sight of boys playing soccer in the courtyard beyond their window.

"Why aren't they in school?" Suham asked. "Does school let out in May?"

"They're out because it's Friday," Najat said.

"Oh." Then she wondered why they weren't at home studying, since it was only a few weeks from exams. When she was in Baghdad, she studied harder in high school than her son Fadi did in university.

"What a bright sun," Suham said, her eyes squinting as she faced the window and watched the playground again. She remembered how when she was a teenager walking home from school with her friends, they'd stop and peek at the boys playing soccer. That was how she'd started liking boys, and for her, it had been the nicest stage of a relationship, because it was the quietest.

"What would you like to eat?" the waiter asked.

Suham turned to him, cleared her throat and strained her mind to come up with a quick decision. "Eggs and potatoes."

Rita ordered a plate of fruit, and when Suham told her to eat something more to hold her until lunch, she explained that she terribly missed eating apples and oranges. "We've been deprived of fruit ever since they placed the sanctions on Iraq."

"We were in the middle of celebrating the end of the war with Iran," Najat said, "when news broke that we were about to be bombed."

Najat complained how the war destroyed the poor, how Iraq's money built Jordan's economy, and how hunger had turned her country into a battlefield, with robbery and murder.

"But *youm*, that's all exaggerated," Rita said, addressing her mother. She turned to Suham and described how they'd taken shelter in Mosul, a city in Northern Iraq with mostly Christian inhabitants, when the bombing was going on; how everyone had been asked, for safety purposes, to stay inside their homes until further notice.

"That period lasted only a month or so," Rita said. "After that, my friends and I didn't have a problem going anywhere."

"That wasn't because Baghdad was safe, it was because you were cautious," Najat said, firmly. She then described how, every time one of her sons came home, either one of her children, or she herself, would stay in the house and keep an eye out for intruders while her son would drive his car into the garage and await a family member to come and escort him into the house.

"But not together," Najat said. "We never walk together, so if one is attacked, the other could help."

"*Youm*, that's all true," Rita said. "But honestly, Baghdad is not unbearable."

"To us it's not, because thanks to your father, may God rest his soul, we can afford everything. But to others –" Najat did not continue, as she tilted her head towards the window and seemed to meditate.

The waiter appeared. He served a plate of sliced apples, oranges, bananas and strawberries to Rita, and a plate of eggs with something or another for everyone else. After tasting it, Rita complained the fruit here wasn't half as delicious as it was at home.

"Baghdad's fruits taste like honey," she said.

Suham smiled, re-tasting the figs she'd eaten from a paper bag while sitting in the car that drove her out of Baghdad and into Jordan when she last visited. A peaceful drift seemed to embrace their breakfast table. No one dared to utter a sound and disrupt the others' spirits. And in the midst of this magical sensation, Michael laughed.

Her eyes widening, Rita smiled and she asked him if she'd said something funny.

"No," he said, seeming more surprised by her question than she had been by his behavior. And he continued to laugh, but more quietly this time.

They'd planned on leaving the hotel right after breakfast, but Rita said she needed to change her shoes before they went anywhere. They took the elevator to the fourth floor, and while Rita and her mother walked down the hallway, Suham and Michael stood against the wall and awaited their return.

Michael peeked further into the hallway, even though it was empty, and then he asked his aunt to step aside, where no one could hear them, so he could tell her something.

"What's the matter?" she asked, hoping that Rita hadn't in some way offended him, that it was a simple case of him finding a smut on her shoulder and hating it.

He didn't reply, but walked further to the left and sat on a small couch between the elevators. His head dropped a few inches, and he exasperated her more in one minute than George did in a whole day. She could not figure out what was the matter with him, but thought it safe to keep as quiet as a butterfly.

When he lifted his head, he looked at her in despair, as if he'd dropped the *maqloubi*, an elaborate dish of spiced cauliflower and onions on the bottom half and plain white rice on the top half, that looked like a cake when turned over onto a tray. Michael drew her all sorts of pictures with his face to hint what was wrong, but they were as abstract to her as geometry.

"I just realized the strangest thing," he said.

That you went to school with Rita in the first grade and she'd been as popular with boys as hair ribbons were with girls, Suham wanted to tease, but didn't.

"Rita reminds me a lot of Nisreen, her eyes especially."

Suham sighed with relief. For a second, she'd worried Rita had invited him to her bed, or that she made fun of his nose, or she had insulted his intelligence. "Doesn't she though? That beautiful smile, and the delicate way she ate the fruit..."

"No, no," he interrupted, seeming perturbed. "That's not what I mean. I mean, Nisreen is like a sister to me."

"Yes, but Nisreen is beautiful."

"Yes, but Nisreen is like my sister."

"But Nisreen isn't your sister!"

"It doesn't matter what she is, it's what she feels like."

Suham frowned as she moved away from him and glanced down the hallway to see whether Rita and her mother were coming. Keeping in mind what she had to deal with, she exercised her patience before she returned to Michael.

"Tell me, Michael, does Nisreen feel like a sister

because of her full cheeks and little nose, or because she was put in your lap the day she was born?"

"I don't know, but –" He pressed his palms against his forehead. "You don't understand. I can't get romantically involved with Rita."

"Because she reminds you of Nisreen?"

He looked at her like she was the crazy one. "Yes, because she reminds me of Nisreen!"

Suham laughed with sarcasm. "That's interesting, Michael. You meet a girl for the first time, and she feels like a lover one night and a sister the next morning?"

He hid his face in his hands and loudly sucked in air. Suham sat beside him and gently stroked his hair, the way she would a silk fabric. She discouraged him from thinking such wicked thoughts, and asked him not to make decisions until more time had passed.

"We can't talk right now, *habbibi*," she said, hearing the ladies' voices coming from the hallway. She smiled down at him. "Nisreen will laugh a good deal when she hears this."

Rita came around the corner with a bright smile.

Suham forced herself to smile in return. "You're ready?"

"Yes." Then Rita's eyes dropped towards Michael's direction, and her smile began to lose its glow. "Is something wrong?"

Michael didn't reply, so Suham quickly intervened. "No, nothing," she said. "But we'd better hurry and find an apartment before it gets late."

When they got downstairs, they found Saad in the lobby. He'd been waiting there since eleven o'clock.

"Why didn't you join us for breakfast?" Suham asked.

"I didn't want to impose."

"Well, next time, impose."

Najat said she couldn't handle going around the city from one taxi cab to the next in order to find apartments, so she asked them to pick her up from Hannan's house when they were all done.

The taxi drove them to half-a-dozen cities, from Jabal Al-Hussein to Jabal Al-Amman. They wanted a two-bedroom apartment to rent for a few months. Saad had already searched the newspaper and had asked friends where he could find a reasonably priced apartment with good accommodations. The first he took them to was located in Jabal Al-Hussein.

Suham had fallen in love with it, but Rita objected to it not having air-conditioning.

"But Rita, it's on the fifth level, and it has windows all around," Suham said, walking from one corner of the apartment to the other. The cool breeze felt so nice it would've put Suham to sleep faster than steamed milk could. After all, they were on a *jabal*, mountain.

"Jordan's air is heavenly," the landlady said. "It never gets hot enough for air-conditioning."

"I guess it's alright," Rita said, still sounding displeased. "But why don't we look around some more? The bathrooms are a little dirty. And the neighborhood –" She peeked through the window to an eerie scene of old buildings and grubby men, and shuddered.

Their hunt continued towards more fancy cities, which were as quiet as the desert and as clean as a washed cup. Extravagant places did not impress Suham, because she worried that she'd leave a shoe mark when she walked on their mopped floors and upset the mistress.

"Besides, I already live in solitude," Suham said

to Saad. "Why would I want to vacation in one as well?"

But then she figured she ought to be more reasonable, since Rita had been born in luxury. If someone were accustomed to eating Arabic cuisine every day, how would they react when suddenly served a hot dog on a bun?

With the sun hot on their heads, they went up and down hills, Rita always walking beside Suham and Michael always ahead of them, walking at a faster pace beside Saad.

"What's wrong with Michael?" Rita asked.

Suham watched Michael speed, as fast as if he was avoiding the Jordanian police. "Why, what's the matter?" she asked.

"He's not the same as last night," Rita said. "He's running away from me."

Suham observed the distance between them and the men. It was as far apart as if they were at an Arabic party, doing the *depka* at the opposite ends of the line. "I shouldn't be telling you this, Rita, but last night, Michael told me how much he adored you. He was so sincere about it, I had expected him to propose at the breakfast table today."

Rita blushed and bent her head.

"Come on, let's catch up with them."

With Rita behind her, Suham trotted to where the boys were, and she jokingly asked if they'd yet found a clever way to lose them. Saad went into a whole speech about how he hadn't meant to leave them behind, but before he arrived to his conclusion, Suham said, "Well, just in case you do decide to dispose of us, make sure it's some place exciting. Like a disco."

They ransacked three large cities and eleven apartment complexes, and amongst them, they found expensive, dirty, or no-vacancy housing. But the

Chaldeans in America, who'd once lived in Jordan, had assured Suham that "you arrive in Amman in the evening and by nighttime, you find a dozen cheap apartments."

"You heard what the superintendents said," Saad reminded her. "The Kuwaitis and Saudis who vacation here in the summer have already booked everything."

They walked for miles, and Rita whimpered about never having traveled on foot so much in all her life.

"Didn't you ever ride the buses in Baghdad?"

"No, I always had a car or a chauffeur."

Suham wondered why Rita would want to leave such luxury, to leave her family, and to reside in Wadi's house. Over the phone, Suham had been honest in describing to Rita Michael's circumstances in America, that he was wealthy enough to enjoy dining out with his wife once or twice a week, but not wealthy enough to provide for her a maid.

Then Rita cried about being hungry. "Can we stop somewhere and eat, please?"

Neither Saad nor Michael said a word, so Suham tried to rescue Rita's request. "Michael, we should rest, really. At least for an hour."

His hands on his hips, he looked around the city, side to side, like a navigator. "It's better we find an apartment, wait to get back to the hotel, change our clothes, and then eat."

"Your nephew is something else," Rita said as they started walking again.

Then someone directed them to a beige building with purple stripes that reminded Suham of one of her niece's Easter dress. It was clean and charming and was worth the $900 a month.

Saad beside him, Michael asked the superintendent at the front desk what sort of deposit was needed for the apartment, while the ladies stood a few feet behind him.

"How long do you plan on staying?" the man asked.

"Maybe a few weeks, maybe a few months," Michael said. "I'm really not sure."

Suham pushed herself to the front desk, and tapped Michael, who hadn't taken notice of her, on the shoulder. "A few weeks, Michael?"

"I figure we'll get something temporary, and if we end up staying in Jordan, we'll either renew our contract or find another apartment."

"If we stay?" she asked, tightly. Because all eyes were on her, she couldn't unleash her anger and make a scene that would need an army troop to stop.

"It's better this way, trust me," Michael said. "So we don't waste money in the hotel."

"Why should we move twice?" She was trying her best to behave as casually as he was. "We have twelve suitcases to deal with."

"I think your aunt is right," Rita said with great discretion, as if she was walking into a gypsy's territory and feared being bitten by a snake.

Michael ignored Rita's comment the way a mother in the middle of a juicy phone gossip did her child's question.

"We'll see," Michael murmured to the air. "Let's just take things slowly – one thing at a time."

The minute they got to their hotel room, everyone rushed to the fruit basket. Michael and Saad rushed out again to take the deposit to the superintendent while the ladies packed their belongings back into the luggage.

When Suham and Rita were left alone, each sat on one bed, across from the window that overlooked the city of Amman. Suham observed the scenery.

"The city is so bright, it's beautiful –"

"Michael is acting strange," Rita said.

"Michael is in the habit of doing that." Suham looked at the phone. "Would you like to order something from the restaurant?"

"No, thank you," Rita said, hastily. "Aside from last night, has he said anything to you?"

"Not at all."

"Hmm," Rita sighed, biting her lips and looking down at her hands. "Please don't feel obligated towards me. If this marriage doesn't go through, I won't be destroyed. I can easily go back to Baghdad and be happy."

"It's not out of obligation that I want this marriage. I love Michael, and I want what's best for him." She paused and looked at Rita. "You are what's best for him. I believe that, and so does everybody else in America."

"What about Michael?"

"I can't speak for him. But here's what I know. He wants things to go slow, because in America that's how relationships work. What we're doing now is too old-fashioned for him."

They were both quiet.

"I can't say he doesn't like me, because over the phone – and last night – he's shown me he does," Rita said. "But now I'm doubting the degree to which he likes me."

"He liked you enough to come all the way to Jordan to meet you."

"I don't know," Rita nearly whispered, bending her head. "Perhaps he doesn't like that I'm already in love with him."

This splashed Suham's face like water. She'd known it was as hard to break Michael's stubbornness with her beliefs as it was to break a walnut with her teeth, but she never suspected that with age, he might become so conceited, he'd snub love. His head had turned into the size of a watermelon.

"Stop anticipating the worst," Suham said with a smile, to cover her worry. "First, let's see what mood Michael is in when he comes back."

Rita smiled too. "If he comes back."

Chapter 14

❧

The ladies lay down on the beds and took a nap. The heat, as well as the little packing that they'd done, had exhausted them. They had dust on their toes and hardened perspiration on their backs. Like a shower, the soft pillow and clean bed sheets soothed Suham, and it reminded her of the time when she worked at the party store, before her first child was born, and after her second child went away to college.

After having worked a six-hour shift between the smells of beer and sausages, Suham would come home to the scents of cardamom and Lysol. She'd wash with heavy perfumed soaps, and after leaving the bathtub, she'd message her legs and arms with a cocoa butter lotion.

George never made her a regular schedule, so Suham showed up to work in spurts; in cases of emergencies, or in-between cashiers. She did not mind the job, but she didn't like the store's policy; there was no limit on the number of empty bottles a customer could cash in, there were too many brands of cereals and too few types of chips.

George listened to her suggestions seriously but he never carried them through. So Suham asked not to be placed on the schedule again, unless he truly needed her, in which case she'd have to come in with a blindfold and some earplugs, and she'd stand behind the register as mute as one of the beach girls on the Budweiser posters.

Her words hurt George more than she'd meant them to, but to make him feel better, she'd gently blown air into his wound. "I'd rather not work for now," she'd told him. "I'm thinking of taking a computer class."

As if it was a winning lottery ticket, George eagerly slipped this idea into his pocket and walked away a happier man. He'd asked her a few months later, when he saw she was neither attending school nor registering for classes, if she'd changed her mind about computers.

"Yes, I have," she'd replied, and then she'd asked him how he liked the fish that she'd fried for dinner that evening.

The men's laughter from the hallway caused enough turbulence to awake both Rita and Suham. The ladies stared at each other as if to ask who they were and what events led them to be in the same room. When their memory returned, they exchanged smiles. Rita yawned out loud, stretched her arms and cuddled closer to the pillow, while Suham turned towards the door. She studied the art of the doorknob teasing the hand, making it jolt right, then left, right again, and left, until it let onto its secret; the other side of the door.

Michael walked in and Saad followed, both still laughing. The humor had to do with three women who, not having been related, had shared a taxi with the intentions of dividing the fare. When it came to paying, however, they'd insulted each other's mathematics abilities and outraged the driver, who wanted his money and his next passengers, Michael and Saad, to get into the cab.

Michael had asked the driver how much they'd owed him.

"*Dinariene*, brother."

After calculating this amount in his head and transferring it to American money, Michael came up with approximately ninety cents per passenger. Laughing amusingly, he'd offered to pay their fare. The women mumbled a few unkind words to each other; they grabbed their grocery bags of vegetables; they thanked and blessed Michael repeatedly, and they stepped out of the taxi into the bustling streets.

"*Ashkurak, ya-iyouni, ya-azzizi, ya-galbi. Nika-thitni!*" The man had thanked Michael, and called him his eyes, his dear, his love, and his heart for having saved him.

They moved into their new apartment, and again Saad and Michael left the two ladies alone, this time to buy a dinner of *tabbooleh, falafel* and shish kebab. In the meantime, Suham and Rita put their strengths together and dragged the luggage into the bedrooms, Suham taking the room with the two twin-size beds and Rita, the one with the king-size bed.

They did not unpack, but did the essential cleaning; washing the dishes that were in the cupboards and the utensils in the drawers, since they planned on eating off of them; and wiping the chairs, the tables and the toilet seat with soap and water. When the work was done, Suham took off her shoes and rested on the couch, while Rita sat on the floor, across from her, and arranged the flowers Saad had brought to the airport into an empty vase she'd found near the refrigerator. Suham picked up the phone, called the front desk, and asked the receptionist if she knew the country code for America. "It's 00 –"

Suham wrote it down on paper, repeated it to the lady, then dialed the country code, followed by the area cold and Wadi's home number. She picked up on the second ring.

"*Allou! Allou!*"

Wadi was as happy to hear Suham's voice as she had been when she first found out that Suham had given birth to a baby boy. Before they talked of the wedding, Wadi asked four or five times about her sister and son's well being, bidding Suham to tell Michael to take good care of his aunt, and for her, his aunt, to take good care of him.

"You ought to be more concerned about yourself, Wadi, than you are about us," Suham said. She then explained to her how with Saad's help, and God's generosity, they were in the best of care.

"Rita is beautiful," Suham said, when Wadi inquired about the bride-to-be. "The first day Michael saw her, he wanted to marry her. Today he's being moody, though, because she reminds him of Nisreen."

Wadi called Michael foolish; that Rita resembling a girl as divine as Nisreen was all the more reason for him to adore her. "He always had bad taste," she said and compared Rita to the American girl she'd found in her house the one Sunday morning.

"He also says that she's short," Suham said. "But I told him that wasn't a problem, considering she's blessed with every other quality."

Rita's eyes met Suham's, and they exchanged a friendly smile before she returned to arranging the flowers again.

"Is she terribly short?" Wadi inquired about Rita's height as if it was her reputation.

Suham didn't take her sister's concerns as seriously as she would have in Michigan. *"La itdeerien bal, la itdeerien bal,"* she said, and prayed that Wadi would take her advice and not worry.

Before they hung up, Wadi gave her regards and blessings to Rita and asked Suham to kiss her on both cheeks, on her behalf. In return, Suham told Wadi to kiss her nieces and her nephews, and her daughter and son, on her behalf. "And tell George I'll call him soon."

The men came home late, having stopped at the supermarket to buy eggs, cooking oil and bread. Suham was impressed that they'd taken such a feminine matter into their own hands, but she wished they would've completed it with tea or coffee.

The four of them sat on the floor, around the table. They did not use the dishes Suham and Rita had washed, eating instead out of the bags and plastic containers the food came in. Suham enjoyed this simple dinner as much as she would've Huntington Palace's extravagant ones. The many side orders of olives, parsley, eggplant puree, *homous* and tomatoes on the table, the rare apartment environment, and the carefree way in which she scooped the food with bread, made her forget that in another country, on the same planet, she was a wife who knew how to cook.

The quantity of the food had filled their stomachs so much that after they rubbed their hands together to wipe the cooking flour off them – having used bread as utensils – they wanted to sleep. But Saad had to catch the last bus to the city where he lived and worked, and they had to pick up Najat from Hannan's before it got late and she began to worry.

Michael, however, ended up falling asleep on the couch. Suham put a pillow beneath his head so his neck wouldn't ache and a cover over his body so he wouldn't get cold. Standing over him, neither she nor Rita had the heart to wake him up.

"Let's pick up my mom on our own," Rita said. "I know the way."

Suham looked at him, and as if Rita could read Suham's worry that he'd wake up and wonder where everyone was, she said, "He'll still be asleep by the time we come back. You wait and see."

The taxi couldn't find the address, even with Rita's help. And he ended up dropping them off in the wrong area, because Rita had pointed to a yellow building with a blue sign and ordered him to stop. "It's only a few minutes away from here by foot."

They went down, walked one block to the left and asked directions, and they walked one block to the right and asked directions. But no one was able to guide them with success. They eventually led themselves to a dark empty street, where an occasional car passed by.

One car slowed down as it approached them and the driver said, "Why have two moons come down from the sky today?" Another driver, in another car said, "Thank God a thousand times for making such behinds." Some guys cried in anguish, others whistled, and most just honked their horns.

Arm-in-arm, their heads as high and as straight as the movie projectors in cinemas, Suham and Rita rushed to find a more lighted and populated area. They finally found a mini-market, and giggling like teenage girls who'd just ran into the boys they liked, they asked the man behind the register for directions. He gave it to them as confidently as if he'd been asked the price of a milk carton.

Suham and Rita bought chocolates from Switzerland and ate some on the way to Hannan's house. Suham thought that had she been an unmarried teenager for a longer time, this was how she would have spent every day.

"This is a very nice apartment," Najat said, turning left and right while standing in the center of the apartment, like a broken ceiling fan that could only spin halfway.

"It's in a secluded area, though." Suham imagined how George, had he been in Amman, would've rented any apartment she'd chosen. When they were looking for homes years ago, and the real estate agent would give them tours of houses, emphasizing the main features, like the new kitchen tile or the insulated windows, George would look at Suham for her reaction before he gave any feedback to the agent. He never permitted himself to be happy, before she first smiled.

"They haven't forgotten anything, have they?" Najat asked, looking into the cabinets and drawers. "Rita, bring the spices from the blue luggage."

Najat had brought one of the eight suitcases in Hannan's house, which emitted two dozen smells; curry, sumac, pepper, turmeric, thyme mixture, verjuice, tea leaves. Rita and Najat sniffed some of the bags and opened others to distinguish between the salt and sugar. They tucked the least used ingredients into the cupboards and laid the common sugar, salt and pepper on the counter beside the stove.

Neither the noise nor the spices had woken Michael up, so Suham nudged his shoulders. "Go change and sleep on the bed, *habbibi*."

He staggered into the room and she returned to help Rita and Najat clean up the dust of the spices and grains by sweeping the floors and wiping the counters.

They washed their hands, turned the kitchen lights off, and sat on the couch to watch television. Then Michael opened the door and, sticking only his head out, asked if he could have a word with his aunt.

Rita and her mother did not stir a lash. Suham quietly left her seat and joined Michael. The air in the room felt as sticky as that in Amman's airport. She opened the windows, looked outside, and seeing only a long empty street, she missed her neighbor Lisa. She hoped Nisreen would open the windows if she fried something like *iroog* for her father.

Michael hadn't said a word and she understood he wanted her to initiate the talk. "What's the matter?"

"I'm fucked!"

She raised her brows. "Do you want me to make you a cup of tea?"

He looked at the ceiling and twisted his right earlobe, like she did to each *kiliecha's* dough trimming, to seal the crushed walnut and sugar stuffing inside it.

"I need time," he said.

Her lips puckered, she nodded her head. "I guess I shouldn't have suggested last night that you get married in one week."

She leaned against the closet, folded her arms in front of her and asked him if he had a cigarette. He said he didn't.

"Hmm, I was depending on Saad for them," she said. "I should never depend on anyone for anything." Except for George. He'd reserve his name months in advance and could always be called upon when she needed a favor.

"Is this the only thing you wanted to say to me?"

He didn't respond.

She knew he wanted to say worse things, but that

he, in turn, knew she'd be as hard on his ideas as Baghdad's schools were on girls who didn't cut their nails or boys who didn't comb their hair. He didn't dare. She quietly walked to the bed and settled herself inside the covers.

"Go to sleep, Michael," she said. "And stop thinking. Tomorrow morning, things will be different."

"Maybe you're right."

"Goodnight, Michael."

"Goodnight."

Chapter 15

❧

There was a water shortage when Suham lived in Amman years back, because Jordan could not take its water from the Dead Sea, nor draw it easily from Aqaba. The water tanks in each home couldn't hold enough to bathe frequently in each week, and if one lived where Suham had, they'd sometimes miss their turn altogether. Sharing a dwelling with two other families, which made a total of six people, Suham once borrowed water from the neighbors, husband and wife, heated it in a pot over a fire, and carried it to the bathtub with her.

Curled in a fetus position, she'd pour a bucket of water over her head, feel it slither behind her back and drip over her toes and nipples. She'd dream about the steaming hot baths she'd be having in America, with bubbles and lather. She'd wrap a pink towel with white ribbons around her wet body afterwards, and then she'd sit beside a fireplace with a cup of cocoa and whipped cream, and she'd read a magazine until her husband came home and saw this view.

This dream was ruined when she'd entered her home in Michigan and realized that not only did it not have a usable fireplace, but it was going to be shared with her in-laws. "It'll only be for a year, and then we'll move into our own place," George promised her, and characteristically, kept his promise.

In these recent days in Amman, Suham hadn't experienced water shortage, but today the douche in the shower had turned cold on her. She wiped the soap off her body with a towel and rinsed the shampoo in her hair inside the sink. She stepped out of the bathroom shivering.

"How quickly everyone showered before me this morning," Suham said.

"No one showered before you, except for those damn spoons and dishes you guys had washed all day," Michael said, his eyes on the television screen.

She kept a towel on her hair and sat down beside Michael. They were watching Younis Shalebi try to befriend a plain girl in order to get closer to her stunning sister, when Najat came out of the bedroom, with a towel and brush in her hands.

She smiled at them. "Good morning."

"Good morning."

Suham hoped that she planned on only washing her hands and face, since she'd finished the hot water. Suham and Michael returned to watching television.

A few minutes later, Rita opened the same bedroom door her mother had come out of. "Michael, can I see you in private, please?"

He obediently walked inside and closed the door. Suham's heart was stuffed with as much curiosity as a kiwi was with black seeds. She felt uneasy letting Michael sit inside that room, because she knew that without cheat sheets, he would fail the test Rita was about to give him.

Najat came out of the bathroom and as she walked to the kitchen, she fussed about the difficulty in having traveled to a foreign country with one dress and no money. "It's no use showering if I'll wear this

again," she said. "I'll see if I can find something else
to hold me while this gets washed and dried."

Suham turned off the television set and joined
Najat in the kitchen. "Aren't you going to have breakfast?" she asked, seeing her pour tea into a cup.

She sat down on the kitchen table. "I prefer
cheese and marmalade, or cereal with milk, or butter
and honey over eggs."

"We haven't had the chance to go to the market
yet," Suham said, apologetically. "We'll have more
groceries by this afternoon."

"Oh, do not concern yourself with me." Najat
conducted herself like a queen, even though she wore
the same dress every day. "I wish you would've visited
our home in Baghdad."

"Yes, that would have been an experience. But I'd
only sat with Rita for a cup of tea and thought nothing
of it. Until six months ago, she'd been as far away
from my mind as India."

Najat smiled. "God moves the world the way you
do your wedding ring. It's that simple, yet that fun."

There was a long silence between them, with just
the sound of their lips sipping tea. They heard laughter coming from Rita's bedroom. Najat looked toward
it, her features as serious as her deceased sergeant's
would have been in war.

"For the heartache she's caused many decent
men, she is now paying a price."

Suham felt this applied to her rather than Najat's
daughter, and she was suddenly frightened. Suham
might not have been sent on this mission to marry
off Michael but learn a lesson; to appreciate George's
love.

They heard more laughter, louder this time.

"We plan on going to the market today," Suham
said.

"That'll be nice, but I'm afraid you'll have to go alone with Rita."

"Oh?" Suham was taken by surprise, but desperately tried not to show it.

"Once I'm done drinking my tea, I thought I'd pay my cousins a visit."

"Of course."

"Rita tells me the two of you have gotten along quite well, so I trust she'll be good enough company."

"Yes, yes."

This was not a good sign. The laughter that had come from behind the bedroom doors seemed not to have affected Najat at all. But to dwell on Najat's indifference would be no better than to cry over having put too much salt in a pot of rice and tomato paste. Besides, if she talked enough sense into him, Michael could still fix things, just as easily as he had ruined them.

They heard Rita's and Michael's voices at the door and then the guilty party appeared, dressed in his usual grin. Najat excused herself from the table and disappeared into Rita's room, giving Suham the freedom to question Michael on what had been said while she went to do the exact same thing with her daughter.

She scrambled two eggs for Michael, and asked him to repeat the details of his conference. He treated her questions as he did anything that was exposed to germs, very cautiously, without words. She turned off the stove and seasoned the eggs with salt and pepper, then neatly folded a thick rag that sat by the sink, placed it on the kitchen table and set the frying pan on it, so it wouldn't burn the table.

"You must have been horrible to her."

"I told her that she can stay in Jordan longer, to visit Aqaba and Petra, you know," he said. "Not just necessarily to get married."

She blinked her eyes with disbelief.

"I figure if we got attached to each other, I can't go my way, and she can't go hers. It's a mess, really."

She handed him pita bread and refilled her cup with tea before she sat down across from him. He ate the eggs without a problem, whereas she could barely swallow her tea. He had no idea how much damage he was causing himself and everyone else.

"If there's a chance you'll get attached to Rita, then you have feelings for her?"

His faced turned the color of the Marlboro cigarette pack. "I could get attached to a football game after I watched its first quarter, but I'm not going to buy the team and live with them for life!"

"Swallow, *habbibi*, swallow," she said in the calmest manner. "The last thing I want to tell Wadi is that her son choked on a yolk."

As he let the food down his throat, he asked for water. She went to the sink, allowed the water to run until it turned cold, and filled a glass. He gulped it down like it was a shot of tequila.

"Please don't choke on the water, either," she said. "It'll put me in an even worse position with your mom."

Najat came out of the bedroom, holding her purse underneath her arm.

"You want me to help you find a taxi?" Suham asked.

Najat had her hand on the door knob already, fixed on running as far away from Michael's ill actions as her feet permitted. "No need to bother, I'll manage fine."

They said their goodbyes and Najat left.

Suham wrinkled Michael's cheeks between her hands. "You have spooked the poor woman."

"And she didn't even thank me, damn her!"

Suham smiled, when she wasn't supposed to, and she roughed up his hair. "I will now go where the news is less vague."

He grinned. "It might be less vague, but it'll baffle you a whole lot more."

Suham knocked on the door, but did not await an invitation before she entered Rita's room. Rita lay sideways on the bed, dressed in a royal blue silk robe that came up to her knees. Her hair fell over her right shoulder, nearly touching her breasts, and her waist curved like an eggplant.

Rita hadn't used the bathroom yet to wash her face or brush her teeth, but she looked as fresh as the ocean's waves. She glowed, despite the dreadful conversation she'd had with Michael. Suham sat on the bed beside her.

"Your nephew is deeply confused."

"Yes, it does seem like it, doesn't it?"

"He is like a child who enjoys games more than money or power," Rita said. "If I wanted to entice him towards me, I could. But that is not what I want to do. If he'd give me a chance, I'd like simply to love him."

This girl was more courageous than Spartucus, to want to love someone as difficult as Michael.

"He lacks maturity," Rita said. "He says that maybe he'd like me better if I colored my hair and gained a few pounds."

What started out as a restrained smiled lead Suham to laugh. But she was capable of stitching her lips to their original seriousness, as fast as she did the lamb's skin after she'd stuffed it with rice and meat. "I'm sorry, but you really have to know Michael's personality to appreciate his humor."

"Oh, I know his humor very well," Rita responded

with a smile. "As a matter of fact, I think I've fallen in love with it." Touching the belt around her robe, her smile faded, and she became solemn. "But I don't believe it's all humor. It is a way of him speaking the truth."

They looked earnestly at one another, without a word.

"He says you guys are cornering him into this marriage," Rita said. "And so is my family."

"If that was the case, wouldn't you have felt it?" Suham asked, passionately. "Did any of it seem fake on the phone?"

"No, and that is what's killing me. And that is what's – keeping me, too."

"Bear with Michael's moods, please Rita. I want this marriage as badly as you do, because I believe, from the bottom of my heart, that the two of you were destined for one another."

Michael hid himself in his room for hours, as did Rita. Suham didn't have any complaints about their peculiar behavior, because she needed a chance to rest her nerves, especially since she'd had no cigarettes or Turkish coffee.

She did not rest, however, by sitting down, but by wiping the spotless cabinets, sweeping the kitchen floor, scrubbing the wall corners, and disinfecting the bathtub. With Michael in the bedroom she could not unpack. And with Rita in her bedroom, she could not go grocery shopping.

Later in the afternoon, Saad stopped by and saved her. She'd run out of chores, she didn't have cigarettes, she couldn't drink Turkish coffee, and she couldn't sit by the window overlooking Charleston Street. Therefore, she appreciated Saad's company as she did the smells that reminded her of Baghdad. She made him a fresh pot of tea and not having anything else in the refrigerator, cooked him eggs, before she sat down and invited herself to one of his cigarettes.

"Can you get me a pack today?" she asked.

"I can get some right now if you want."

"No, don't." She poured tea into her cup and leaned against the kitchen counter. She blew cigarette smoke into the air, sipped tea, and took more cigarette puffs. She sensed her behavior made Saad feel uncomfortable, because he avoided looking at her.

"Michael is having doubts. A great deal of them."

To show his concern, the bread he was about to put in his mouth changed its route back to the table. But Suham did not want a dramatized reaction, she only wanted a solution. She filled Saad in on what had happened that morning.

"Can you talk some sense into him?"

"You needn't worry," he said, most sincerely. "What you've asked of me goes without saying."

"Yes, well, be subtle about the advice you give him. Michael likes to break other people's word, just for the fun of it."

Saad nodded his head in agreement. Men became very obedient when the issue did not deal with their own lives, she thought, whereas women were the opposite; if it had to do with their family or future, they rolled down their carpets and offered fruit and sandwiches; if it didn't, they pulled their veils closer to their noses, turned their backs, and walked away.

Chapter 16

The sound of the wind outside reminded Suham of a time when she'd loved her husband most. Fadi was barely a year old that autumn, and she had surprised George with tenderness. She'd touched his hand before he touched hers, restrained herself from eating dinner until he arrived home after midnight, and told him she loved him before he said it.

George had been so pleased by the attention he did not ask what had caused it, in case she would come to her senses and return to her frigid ways. But he'd done worse. He started being so nice to her that she'd lost interest in this love mode again. He called her from the store while she did the laundry, or sliced zucchini circles, or changed diapers. He traced her whereabouts, and called there.

Once he called her at her sister-in-law's house, where the ladies had met for brunch, just to tell her how a man came into his store to sell him a spray that was meant to wipe off any stain, ten dollars a bottle, or two for eighteen. "He poured ink on a white sheet of fabric," he'd told Suham over the phone, "sprayed that stuff over it, and rubbed it with a regular cloth. The ink came off instantly."

"I hope you didn't buy it, George."

"I did. Two bottles."

Then he went on to tell her how when he'd tried the same stunt the man had done, he couldn't remove the ink spot from the fabric. "It was a hoax!" he'd laughed.

Then he gave a lengthier account of this incident, furnishing it with more credit than it deserved. George interpreted it with amusement, while she found it absurd. If anyone tried to come into the store and sell her something, she'd give them one mean stare and say, "No, thank you".

But that wasn't the point. George could've waited until he got home to narrate this story of fraud. She'd thought his attachment to her was unhealthy and, at times, annoying. So she'd returned to her old ways, as quickly as she'd abandoned them.

George noticed the difference and questioned why she didn't wait up to have dinner with him lately, or why she didn't tell him she was going to his sister's house for coffee. "*Habbibi*, I try to stay up, but the older your children are getting, the more they wear me out," she'd said to him, stroking his face. "And as for going to your sister's for coffee – you know how I hate bothering you while you're at work."

It being her specialty, Suham had found an excuse for every behavior, and an answer to every question.

Saad took Michael downtown to visit some friends, while Suham took Rita to the supermarket for groceries. Despite the wind outside, Suham insisted that they walk. "You must learn to be as strong physically as you are emotionally."

The tri-level supermarket was like a mall with a produce section. The first floor specialized in coffees, seeds and nuts, breads, fruits, vegetables, packaged food, beauty supplies, and house products. The second floor was designed for clothes and appliances, and the third floor was for electronics.

They shopped for the necessary items, as well as assorted chocolates for unexpected guests, and ending up with twenty-four bags, they took a taxi back home. Suham cooked spinach stew, and while she simmered the meat in the pot and washed and drained the spinach well, she handed Rita the task of pealing the garlic and squeezing the lemons.

The men arrived after seven o'clock, and everyone sat down to eat dinner, this time at the kitchen table. They told each other jokes and exchanged stories. Rita told of days when Baghdad's streets were flooded with two feet of water after a severe thunderstorm.

"My friends and I got extremely bored after not going out of the house for three days," she said. "Then one of the girls rescued us. She managed to find a truck to pick everyone up, and we decided, all eleven of us, to meet at someone's house for tea."

Suham told of how her mother used to hide the *kiliecha* beneath her bed, until Easter or Christmas would come, so her children wouldn't eat it all. "We would've snuck into my mother's room and stole a few pieces," Suham said. "But she always locked the door with a key and placed the key in her brassier."

Saad described how hard his teachers were on him. He'd been a bad student who did not do his homework, did not listen to the teachers, and skipped class. "Once my math teacher put pencils between my fingers and squeezed my hand hard, until he had my whole body arching like a banana."

He laughed at the memory, and so did everyone else.

"And the principal always slapped my hand with the ruler that was made from pomegranate trees, the roughest kind of rulers – besides the metal ones, of course."

Michael was the least sociable one of the company, and he was only an attentive listener to his aunt and cousin, but not to Rita. And it got worse while they were drinking their cardamom tea, when the tension between him and Rita began to thicken faster than oatmeal over a fire.

Saad left before the oatmeal exploded and plastered itself all over his shirt, shoes and pants. He used the excuse, however, that he didn't want to miss the last bus going home.

Suham took the dirty dishes from Rita's hands and placed them in the sink. "Have you talked to your mother at all today?"

"No." Rita went to get the rest of the dishes.

"Won't she find it odd that we didn't pick her up?"

"I think she now expects it."

This was getting messier for Suham than eating *pacha* was for a girl, especially since this elaborate dish was served during special occasions, when girls wore the most lipstick; undoing the tough black threads that held the stuffing together, pulling hard with her teeth to tear the sheep's skin apart, grinding each bite for well over five minutes to avoid choking, then starting all over with the next piece. And any girl was in real trouble if she helped herself to a second serving.

Michael wasn't any kinder towards Rita the following morning. When he went into the kitchen and she happened to be there, he greeted her with his chin in his chest. He ate his fried eggs and tomatoes on the couch in front of the TV instead of at the kitchen table where she was having her tea. He watched the comedy program as soberly as one would a murder mystery.

Suham gazed at him and suddenly wondered whom he'd taken after. Until now, she'd thought he was a male version of herself. She'd been wrong, though. He resembled his great uncle, from his father's side, who'd married twice and had gone through life like it was a casino, taking risks without a break.

When Michael finished his breakfast, he retired to his room. Rita's eyes had followed his every move, and once he disappeared, she stood up, angrily banged her cup of tea on the table and flew off to her room as well. She came out a minute later, wearing black stretch pants and a yellow sweater, carrying her purse over her shoulder and a plastic bag in her hand. "I'm leaving."

Suham tapped her hands on her skirt, to wipe away the soapsuds. "Please, Rita, don't."

"I have to." Rita's voice was very confident and more so impatient. "I don't think me sitting in front of him is doing any good. Maybe if I went away for a few hours, he'll think better."

Suham saw there was no use in trying to change the girl's mind. There was no justice to it, either. Rita had more of a right to leave this house than she herself did to desert her husband by spending Saturday nights at Wadi's. And anyway, perhaps it was true that Michael might think better in Rita's absence.

"Well, do as you like," Suham said. "But expect us to pick you up at night, for dinner."

"That's not a problem, I'll be ready then. But don't come unless Michael wants to."

Suham nodded her head.

"Goodbye." Rita kissed Suham on both cheeks and left.

The instant Rita walked out, Suham burst into Michael's room with a loud noise, like drum. "Rita left."

He looked up at her with as serious an expression as her own. She noticed a feather, however, starting to tickle his stomach and then his throat. He smirked, then smiled, and he posed that way for as long as possible before he slipped on soap and laughed.

"Michael, I'm telling you Rita left."

"Alright, I'm sorry," he said, but his eyes were still sly. "So where did she go, to find a veil at the bazaar, or to visit a friend in prison?"

He laughed so hysterically he pressed his hand on his stomach and twisted his body like a grapevine.

She shook her head, rage cooking her insides. "You are testing my patience, Michael, and I swear on my mother's grave, I will start on you the way I have with my brothers, my husband, and my son, if you don't undo this wreck."

With each word she hurled at him, his face lost its merriment. Her mind raced.

"I've been lenient with you because I trusted that after puberty, you'd behave like a gentleman, on your own. Now I wish I would've been more of an aunt and crushed that vanity you've cultivated, so you wouldn't zoom here and there like a bullet!"

Like a hungry wolf, she'd devoured whatever joy seemed to remain inside of him. All he had left to show was depression, the appropriate reaction at a time like this.

"You took this girl's heart and stained it with your meanness," she continued. "And I don't want to ask for what reasons, Michael, because I already have this horrible feeling that you're sacrificing your future for a few more nights at the bar."

"The bar is not any worse than an unhappy

home," he said, trampling all over his depression. "I want to take my time. I feel suffocated."

She laughed, sarcastically. "If you think you'll suffocate any less by being a jackass, you're wrong. Your stomach can only eat hot peppers for so long before it goes up in flames. And once you're on fire, don't think you'll be able to distinguish curry from honey."

He closed his eyes and dropped his head, and if he would have knelt on the ground, he would've looked exactly like the men in Mosques.

"You'd better start digesting something sweet," she said, harshly, "or else you'll forever forget its taste."

This meditation of his irritated her, and she took a deep breath. "I hope you haven't taken this whole thing this far just so you can sit on the bed and watch me dance in front of you like a gypsy. Speak, please."

His eyes opened. "About what?"

"If you had front row seats to this cinema, like I do, you wouldn't attempt to fool me by pretending to be naïve. You would offer me seeds and nuts so I could tolerate you better."

He went back to his silence, and she to her preaching, with arms folded beneath her breasts. "If there's one thing I hate it's a man who doesn't respond to an argument! With George, it's the same way—I am always the pen and he is the paper."

"Poor George!"

She squinted while tightening her lips. "Look Michael, we really can't afford to sit on Jordan's mountain for the rest of the summer and count stars."

He rubbed his forehead, looking as noble as a chemist. "See, it's tricky. One minute I like her, another minute I don't. I never felt this way about anything before, except for Lipsticks."

She was confused. "What?"

"It's a bar. It's really nice, but sometimes I'd rather be at Wild Woody's or Industry's. See the crowd in each place is different –"

He explained at length how one was popular for the sleaziest girls on earth, while the other was his friends' hangout place, and another had the best dance floor, accentuated by lights, smoke, a stage, stairs, and sometimes a singing band. He described how one was happening on Thursday nights, another on Saturday nights.

Suham slowly paced back and forth, like a teacher with a ruler hovering over a D student. "So are you telling me you flipped a coin on whether or not to keep Rita?"

"Yeah, sort of."

She rolled her eyes and exasperated. "And are you happy now, my dear nephew?"

"Not really." He stared at the ceiling, at the window, at the bed. "Is she mad at me?"

"Not enough to slam the door in your face if she saw you."

He bounced on his feet, as quickly as Arabic ladies unshelled seeds. "Should we go to her now?"

"We'll pick her up later," she said with a sigh of relief. "We'll have dinner here first."

It would not work for Rita's advantage to have too long a time sitting in the restaurant with Michael, because they needed their privacy more than they did food. Besides, such establishments usually had serious atmospheres. A little Nescafe with a piece of cake, on the other hand, was the most flirtatious setting Suham could think of. She'd call Saad and invite him to come along too, because with him, it would be easier to lose Michael and Rita, who surely needed time alone.

Chapter 17

In the taxi ride to Hannan's house, Michael was serious. Suham took credit for having knocked down his arrogance, like she'd once knocked down the beehive that sat on her tree. The beehive had grown into the size of a cantaloupe and Suham had showered the tree with so much lighter fluid, the gasoline smell lasted for days. She'd lit a match and threw it at the beehive, and at the same time, she'd knocked it to the ground with a broom, because she'd wanted to save the tree from the fire.

The bees attacked then, and frustrated, Suham struck them with the broom, and whenever possible, squished a few of them against the cement and rocks. When George came home, he told her to stop before the bees stung her.

"They've already stung me," she said. The broom went flying frantically in the air, as the bees formed a mushroom around her.

Again George asked her, for her safety's sake, to stop. He'd promised to have the exterminators come and wipe the bees out, even their queen. But Suham didn't listen. She waved the broom in all directions, and loved it, feeling the excitement of being in a war, fighting battles against soldiers to destroy the queen, without the tragedy of killing a human being.

When she'd become as restless as she could force herself to be, she moved away from the tree and observed it. One side of it had a few branches missing.

"Go inside and change," she'd told her husband, breathlessly. "So you can help me clean up this mess."

They picked up the broken branches and stuffed them inside a box. She swept the pathway clean of leaves and dirt and he threw them in garbage bags, tied and placed them near the mailbox.

When she'd shared this story with a relative the following week, the relative had laughed at her. "There's a spray for that sort of stuff that you could've bought. It would've finished them all in seconds."

"Oh." But Suham didn't regret having struggled in her front yard. Actually, she'd enjoyed that evening so much she wished she had to rescue her home from this kind of danger every day. To touch dirt and be stung by bees was the sweetest reminder of life.

Saad knocked on the door. As they waited for someone to answer, Michael glanced at his aunt for a split second. He was about to laugh and make light of the situation when she turned her face the other way.

Despite Michael's crudeness, Hannan's hospitality was no less today than it had been the night they'd arrived to Amman. Her words, as well as everyone else's, were sweeter than syrup and her eyes, like everyone else's, were softer than cashmere.

"I've already eaten dinner," Rita said. "I figured we'd go out for café."

They apologized for having eaten without them, as if they'd originally invited them for dinner and had failed to await their arrival before pouring the rice and cucumber stew, or whatever else they'd cooked, into their plates. They offered to order shish kabob and rotisserie chicken from the restaurant next door, in case their company was hungry.

"No, thank you," Suham said. "We too had our dinner."

Suham, Michael, and Rita sat at Hannan's apartment for as long as it took to drink a cup of Turkish coffee and with it, eat a piece of solid chocolate.

They went to a cafeteria in one of Amman's famous gardens. Michael sat beside Rita, one arm around her shoulders and the other on her knee. Occasionally he'd whisper something in her ear and she'd either smile to it and shyly turn away, or she'd laugh, or she'd say, "Michael, that's not true!"

He turned to his aunt. "Doesn't she look like a big strawberry every time she blushes?"

Suham looked at Rita and smiled. "Stop teasing her."

Each ordered a slice of vanilla cake, with custard and pistachio filling, and a cup of Nescafe. Suham finished her cake as quickly as she could, and then asked Saad if he'd be kind enough to take her for a short walk. They left Michael and Rita sitting alone, and as they strolled about, they found themselves out of the garden and in the street.

"Do you want to keep going?" Saad asked her at the garden's gates.

"Yes, please."

She walked further down the street, towards a busy area that reminded her of Birmingham, a city in Michigan popular for its coffee houses, shopping stores and restaurants. Birmingham's entertainment was mostly geared to the young, its expensive merchandise to the rich, the old, and the sophisticated.

Suham had gone there on only a few occasions, first with her daughter. A couple of months before Nisreen's wedding, she and Suham had gone to every mall and shopping center to prepare her a fresh wardrobe for her new life as a wife.

It was Nisreen's idea to go to Birmingham. For as long as Suham had lived in Michigan, the only thing she knew about this city was that it was located on the west side, until Nisreen revealed to her a hidden secret, and broadened her mind.

"Mom, in downtown Birmingham, people walk in the streets," she'd said, passionately. "They window shop, they ride horse carriages, and if the weather is sunny and gorgeous, they drink their cappuccinos and hot cocoas outside the cafeteria."

Suham never considered a place like that existed in Michigan, because there was no clue that it did. On television, she'd seen thousands of people walk the streets of New York and Chicago, whether in snow or rain, in the darkest nights or in the earliest mornings. But Detroit, when portrayed on the news or in movies, was as quiet as the library.

So when her flight landed in Birmingham's downtown airport, Suham was taken by surprise. It wasn't anything like New York, with men in business suits and bumper-to-bumper taxicabs, nor was it like Chicago, with a more subdued New York scene. But it was enough to make her want to stay there a while, and observe.

"You should see Royal Oak," Nisreen had said, when she saw her mother was impressed. "That place is twice as packed, and three times as extraordinary."

It saddened Suham that as long as she'd lived in Michigan, the only facts she knew about the state, outside of the Chaldean society, and the basic stops, like the grocery stores, clothing departments, and doctors' offices, was that it was shaped like a mitten on the map.

There were no bargains in Birmingham, but nonetheless, since walking in such a busy street without bags would be as boring as sitting in a restaurant and ordering only water, they'd bought Nisreen a casual dark brown dress and matching shoes, a beige sweater, and a silver bracelet. And from a bulk food store, they'd purchased dried apricots and sunflower seeds.

Saad said much about many things, but Suham hadn't heard anything except for the sound of her heels clicking against the pavement as she walked. Her mind had been doing needlework, weaving all sorts of threads and fabric, to make one sense out of her life.

So she often smiled at Saad after realizing he'd finished a sentence, or she said "Really?" when she caught the last few words of his sentence, which were, "and that's what happened." But after a while, seeing that they were heading back to the garden, she put her needlework down and forced herself to start paying attention.

"I've heard rumors that my brother's wife gets upset every time he sends me money," he said. "Is it true?"

He didn't give her a chance to answer before he went on to say, "I know I've needed their help for the last year or so, but I promised Salem I'd pay him back every dollar he spent on me."

"Do you plan to go to Greece and be a refugee?"

"Yes." His voice was low, as if embarrassed.

He must know what was coming, she thought.

"Your brother is doing well in America, but in

America doing well isn't the most comfortable place to be in. If you tilt your oar just a little bit, you might get into trouble. With the bank. With the business. With your wife."

She smiled and so did he.

"I cannot stay here," he said.

"Salem won't let you, anyway."

"I don't mean to cause his family problems – "

He exasperated. "Do me a favor, please, and tell his wife how grateful I am for their help. Assure her that when I get to America, I will work night and day at my brother's store so he can rest and I could repay them."

She promised she would, and they walked on.

"If you do hear that she complains," she said later, "don't take it so personally. She is no different than all the other Chaldeans who send money to their families."

He nodded his head in understanding.

"People there don't feel the pain you go through in order to find work and eat," she said. "And people here don't know what people in America go through to keep up with bills and payments."

He bowed his head, seeming to want her to continue, so she did. "I will talk to her, of course."

"I'm not upset about it or anything."

"She will see you one day and realize she invested her money wisely."

He smiled at the compliment and then turned sad quickly. "I wish I didn't have to take a penny from anyone. My father taught me what it meant to be a man, but he didn't know we'd get bombed and scatter like leaves."

He shook his head and frowned, pained at remembering. "You didn't see Iraq after the war. You don't want to. It'll make you hate life."

Tears stung her nose and eyes. "Not seeing it has already made me do that."

With all her might, she sniffed the air that had a tingle of car fumes and cigarette smoke, and she forced her tears back into her memory box. Then she glanced at the cafeteria facing her, and saw Michael and Rita leaning towards each other, seeming as involved in conversation as she was in other people's affairs.

"That boy worries me sick," she said.

Saad looked at their table. "He'll be alright."

A dark skinned man stood on the sidewalk with a wagon of silver jewelry. Saad greeted the man, whom she knew from his dialect to be Egyptian, and looked at a thick bracelet topped with a black rhinestone and engraved with hieroglyphic.

He touched the tip of it. "How much is this?"

"Seven *dinars*."

"No Saad, please don't," she begged.

But he picked up the bracelet and examined it closely.

"Saad, listen –"

He didn't regard her plea as he bargained for a lower price with the Egyptian. He wanted to pay three *dinars*, but the man swore, on his mother's grave, his Prophet Muhammad, on his own head even, that he couldn't.

"*Ya-zalama,* I'm not lying when I tell you this cost me five *dinars*."

They finally agreed on six *dinars*.

"Only because I'd put Iraqis before my own eyes, and I love Saddam Hussein," he said, laughing. "I lived in Baghdad for fifteen years, *ya-zalama*, doing odd jobs, smelling fresh air."

Saad thanked him for honoring them with such hospitality, and when they walked away from his wagon, he whispered to Suham. "He cheated us because he knew you were from America."

Suham thanked him for the bracelet but left it in the bag. She decided she wouldn't be severe with him for the act he'd just performed, but from now on, she would be cautious.

"What took you guys so long?" Michael asked when they came back.

"I was in the mood to walk," Suham said.

Michael said it was his turn to take Rita for a walk. Before they left, however, Suham showed Rita her bracelet, not because she wanted to, but because Rita had asked to see what was in the bag.

"It's beautiful," Rita said, taking a deep look at it. "*Mabrook*."

"Thank you."

Iraqis congratulated each other from the littlest purchases to bigger events, like passing the immigration test. But in this particular case, Suham felt uncomfortable hearing the word. She felt that it had insulted her marital status, even though Rita had meant it to be a sincere gesture. She figured she'd give this bracelet as a gift to one of her nieces when she got back to Michigan.

With quick steps Michael and Rita went for their walk. Saad and Suham watched their backs move farther and farther away, until disappearing behind the trees and bushes.

Saad smiled. "It looks like they don't want to be anywhere near us."

"Let them run away from us!" she cheered.

"It's a good sign."

Chapter 18

The night dragged on longer than the canals of Venice. She sat on the couch, in the dark, and while smoking a cigarette, replayed the time spent in the gardens. Michael touching Rita's knee, whispering in her ear, Saad buying her a bracelet, she feeling guilty because of it. He'd gone home now, and she was thankful for that, because as with Thai food, she'd enjoyed his company more than she'd expected.

She was about to fall asleep on the couch when Rita appeared, dressed in her blue robe. "Come, keep me company."

Rita sat beside Suham. "Tell me all about Michael."

Suham smiled. She remembered how her children used to leave their beds at night, snuggle, one on each side, between her and George, and beg for a story she'd made up once, about the princess who broke her mother's word by going into a castle made of candle wax. In this castle lived a monster, also made of candle wax, who was so mean, that whenever someone visited him, he'd lock them inside and never let them leave.

"Huh!" her children would gasp, embracing their mother's arms and thighs tighter.

Suham would smile, but continue in a grisly voice. "The princess cried when she knew she'd never see her mother, or her father, or her friends again. But then, to her surprise, every teardrop that touched the candle wax melted it, like it was a lit mach. When the princess noticed what her tears could do, she wringed her eyes, like mommy did your pajamas, so the tears would make a hole in the wall." She took a break, and a breath.

"After she squeezed herself out of the hole and ran away," she continued, "the monster got so sad, he cried and cried and cried, and his tears fell on his face, his arms, his legs, melting away all the candle wax. When he looked in the mirror, he couldn't believe his eyes. He was a handsome prince!"

"Huh!" they gasped with wide, happy eyes.

"He ran out of the castle and went to find the princess," she said, excitedly. "When the princess saw that he was a prince, and not a monster, she fell in love with him. *Oue ashaou isha saeeda.*"

As she'd sing the words "and they lived happily ever after", her children would snuggle closer to her bosom and giggle before falling asleep.

"What would you like to hear?" Suham asked Rita. "How as a young boy, Michael used to compete with his friends on who'd find the most bird's nests?"

Rita smiled. "Will I like living in America?"

Suham sighed, heavily, after taking a puff of her cigarette. "You will. Better than me at least, because you're friendlier. I, on the other hand, can be too rude and arrogant."

"I can't imagine you being rude and arrogant towards anyone!"

Suham laughed, lightly. "I can't imagine you not imaging me rude and arrogant."

Rita didn't argue.

"I used to be worse – to men especially." She extended her hands over the table to search for the pack of cigarette she'd been smoking from. When she found it, she took one cigarette out of it and offered one to Rita.

Rita shook her head. "But thank you."

"I won't condemn you for it."

Rita laughed. "I don't smoke, honest."

Suham nodded her head and started smoking, while staring straight ahead. "I tried to teach my daughter to be like me, but she had too much of a heart. She thinks the world of her husband, and not only because they're newlyweds. She'll adore him for the rest of his life."

Suham turned to Rita. "You will be placed between me and my daughter in the degree of admiration towards your husband."

"I'll adore him completely!"

"Not completely. You have too much of your own mind."

"Which means I can't completely adore a man?"

"Not more than you adore yourself."

Rita thought a little, while her finger traced the hem of her robe. "Because I haven't fallen in love until now?"

"Isn't that enough reason?" Suham grinned as she remembered a crucial point. "Although I can't guarantee you would have been any different if say, you married at sixteen."

Rita tilted her head to the side and curled her hair around her ear. "I've never approved of those girls who sacrifice too much for a man."

"I never have, either. But I wonder, what is too much?"

"Their dignity is too much!"

Suham arched her brows. "And what falls in the dignity category, may I ask? Women like us – or a lady in your case – tend to make an issue out of a smile."

"You speak of our strength as if it's something bad."

"It's not bad, but it has a price."

The following day, the ladies enjoyed cooking okra stew together and eating it together, alone, because Michael went out for dinner with a few of Saad's friends. They returned early, however, so they'd all have ice cream at a café, before Saad would take the last bus home.

The town was as tranquil as a sanctuary, and its melancholy was contagious. Neither the taxi driver nor his passengers uttered in the cab. Even when he parked the car, the driver simply rested his arm over the steering wheel and squinted his eyes out the window.

"Is this the place?" Saad asked.

The driver nodded and waited his fare. Saad paid him while the rest of the group got out and headed toward the cafeteria located at the corner of a main street. The tables in the establishment were white, round, and empty, with the exception of two friends who were smoking water pipes.

Once they were seated, Suham tried to start a conversation about how beautiful the cafeteria was, how surprisingly quiet the town had been, and how good the cool night breeze felt. But Michael stomped on whatever remarks she made by simply nodding his head in agreement.

So Saad took it upon himself to host the table. He told them a story of how in the army he'd befriended the cook who had taken better care of his stomach than his own wife had. "I was the only one who ate marinated chicken and soft bread."

Then he described how skillful his father used to be at repairing typewriters and calculators. And how, from him, he'd learned a lot about electrical equipment. "Because he knew how to fix typewriters, people used to bring him their television sets."

There was an intermission during Saad's narration, as Michael ordered two Nescafe for Rita and Suham, and vanilla ice creams for everybody.

Saad resumed. A story about his brother having stolen a goat, because the lady of the house wouldn't give him permission to ride it. "He'd gotten so angry with her," Saad said, laughing, "that he untied her goat and took it with him miles away."

Suham laughed, as did Michael, saying how they remembered that particular story, because like their skin, it too had immigrated to America with them.

The waiter interrupted their talk when he served the Nescafe with a kettle of steamed milk and a chocolate-coated biscuit. Everyone remained silent after he left. Rita hugged her jacket around her chest as the cool breeze turned into a cold wind, and she brought the cup of Nescafe close to her chin. The steam danced towards her eyes, like a genie coming out of a magic lamp.

Having lived in Michigan as long as she had, Suham tolerated the cold a lot better than Rita. Especially after that one morning on her patio, when she'd learned how such weather was capable of soothing a troubled woman's mind.

The ice cream was more delicious than any dessert she'd tasted in a long while. It was stuffed with chunks of fresh pistachios, and it must have been made with prime milk. Evidently she wasn't the only one who thought so highly of it, because all Michael could talk about for the next fifteen minutes was how incredibly good the ice cream tasted.

He was as delicate with his spoonfuls as a wine tester was with his sips. "This is the best ice cream on earth!"

He continued dwelling on it, forgetting that the quality of Amman's ice cream was not a world affair.

Michael's spoon moved from the bowl to his mouth so quickly it generated a race amongst the utensils. Each spoon moved faster than its neighbor, but in the end, Michael's won. Within minutes, he'd managed to empty the bowl of ice cream, cross the finish line, and land the spoon on the table.

He wiped his mouth with the napkin, set it back down, stared at it, softly tapped his fingers against it, picked it back up, wiped his mouth again, and set it back down. Again he tapped his fingers against the napkin. When this odd ritual ended, he leaned back against the chair and closely observed each person sitting at the table, starting with Saad and going around to Suham. His eyes were willful, his smile subtle, his body firm.

This sight frightened Suham, because she didn't know what to make of her nephew's conduct. For the first time ever, she felt what it was like to be standing in George's shoes. Which reminded her. She hadn't called her husband yet.

Michael's hand went into his pocket, brought out ten *dinars* and set them on the table. "I'm going to catch a taxi."

"You're going home alone?" Suham asked.

"No, I'm just going to catch a taxi."

Suham kept quiet, because if she were to say anything, it would lead to a scene. That had her counting. How many scenes had she prevented from happening so far? Ten, twenty? She decided she'd save them in her memory bank until she arrived to Michigan, then use them.

"You guys follow me whenever you're ready," Michael said and casually walked away.

He stood next to the curb and waited for a taxi. Suham and Rita grabbed their purses from over the table, and Saad put on the leather jacket his brother had sent him from America. They hurried after Michael, and there, they all stood next to each other in silence.

A taxi pulled up at Michael's motion to stop. The seating, aside from Saad's usual passenger seat, was automatically understood; Rita next to the window on the left side of the car, Suham in the middle, and Michael next to the window opposite Rita's side.

No one said a word. It was the scariest ride Suham had ever taken. She rested her head, closed her eyes and prayed in silence. That God would deliver Michael from evil. That He would give her the strength to steer her nephew in the right direction. That –

"Excuse me," Rita said to the driver. "Can you drop me off at Al-Jawhara Street?"

"Al-Jawhara?" he asked. "By Al-Hussein's garden?"

"No, it's on the other side of the Hilton, near the rubber factory."

"Ahhh, yes, yes, the rubber factory. It's a four story building?"

"That's the one."

"Yes, yes, I know where that is." He turned his head to observe the traffic on the right. "I just take a turn here, and a left there." He changed lanes and adjusted his seating position. "Yes, yes, I know where that is."

They arrived at Al-Jawhara within ten minutes. Rita grabbed her purse, gave a fake smile to everyone and said goodbye. The men loitering at the chicken shack stared and whistled at her. She shyly bent her head and went inside the apartment building.

"Now to Al-Ashrafia?" the driver asked Saad.

"Yes," Michael answered.

Once the taxi driver changed gears and drove away, the remainder of the ride for Suham was harder to cope with. Especially with Michael beside her. He really wasn't ready yet for marriage, she thought. George had been right.

The absence of Rita's voice and the smell of okra still lingering inside the apartment made Suham feel empty. "Would you like something to eat?" she asked Saad.

"Tea will be fine."

"Good, because I don't feel well enough to pour rice and stew into a bowl, and serve it."

She walked towards the stove, while Michael went into his room. She poured water into the teakettle, placed it over the fire, and went to the window. "Do you mind making the tea?" she asked. "I don't think I can."

"Of course."

He stood over the stove, waiting for the water to boil.

She leaned against the window seal. "What are the odds of me being happy again?"

He frowned. "What do you mean?" Her head dropped and she gave a sarcastic laugh.

"Suham, you are not responsible for whatever happens to Michael from now on," he tried to convince her. "You did all you can do."

"No, it wasn't enough! He did more!"

He said nothing.

"You can stop trying to console me now," she

said. "I will manage."

She considered calling George, but by the time Saad left, she was as exhausted as the day she'd had her first Christmas dinner. Her home and furniture having been new, she'd treated them as delicately as one did a beaded dress; wiping specs of salt as soon as they fell, following the children as closely as a guard did his prisoner, and never sitting down.

Chapter 19

✤

The next few days were awkward, because Suham performed her duties without any memories, none for Baghdad, or for Michigan. She called on the people whom she had letters or gifts for from family members in America. She also called her husband and apologized for not having contacted him earlier, but that under the circumstances, she'd been too distressed to do the typically normal things. He gave his condolences to the break-up of Michael's engagement and said that he understood about her not calling.

"I was sure, *habbibi*, you would," she said, and couldn't really find much else to discuss with him but her children's welfare, the store conditions, and his health. Although he offered to help.

She was not looking for anyone to comfort her, however. Most people who played the role of consultant did so either to praise their own selves or to acquire credit. In George's case, it was the latter. He wanted to prove to her that he wasn't as vague about civilization as she thought him to be.

Michael's condition grew even worse. He had more fantasies than she did memories, and when he tossed each one in the air, Suham caught it like it was an apple and placed it against her bosom until her arms were full. The rest she watched fall to the ground, dent and rot, as she accepted that her arms and her bosom were not enough to support this many apples.

Michael wanted to visit Petra, and Aqaba, and the Dead Sea. And since he was in the area, he craved a tour of Israel, or one of Turkey. Egypt sounded even better, but a place like that would need a month to visit, not a week. And if he could get to Italy, that would be the ultimate. He wouldn't mind Spain. Or Germany. Maybe England. But not France.

"We have to move out of this apartment first." He glared at each and every one of its walls, as if it was a nasty alley.

In an average situation, Suham would've meddled in her nephew's proposals; she'd question what good there was in changing apartments if they were flying to Israel or Germany the next day; she'd convince him that it was wiser to remain where they were until they returned to America.

But nowadays, she listened to his deranged ideas as easily as she smoked a cigarette. She figured if everything else she'd instilled into him in the past hadn't helped, what good would a few extra suggestions do? It would be like adding salt into bland rice after it'd been cooked for days.

Michael delivered the order form to his real estate agent, Saad, and within a day, he, his aunt, and their luggage were transported into a new furnished apartment. Michael was delirious about the place, and complimented it as often as a man would a girl on their first date. But this phase lasted until dinnertime, when he'd announced his next wish. "Let's go back to America tomorrow."

"Tomorrow!" Suham said. "Why tomorrow?"

"There's nothing to do here."

"Michael, *habbibi*, aren't you tired?" she asked while taking a deep breath, as if to experiment with what being tired looked like.

"Yes. I should've never let you guys get involved in my business," he said. "Now look where I am!"

"Oh, that's terrific, Michael," she said, raising her arms in the air. "You're going to make a war between the family?"

"I don't know. I don't think so."

She observed him with repulsion, and he kept quiet.

"Saad is coming over this evening to take us to a friend's house," she said. "Rest in this room until then. I don't want to see you for a while."

And she walked out.

Rita had left two suitcases behind. Suham hadn't mentioned that they needed to be dropped off, because she still hoped Michael would miss Rita enough to ask her back. But seeing that that was as unlikely as a Muslim eating pork, she pointed out this detail to Saad when he came. "We must take the luggage to Hannan's place first."

Suham secured the luggage's padlocks before permitting Saad and Michael to carry it out. She also helped direct them as they struggled in getting the luggage into the elevators. "Move a little that way," Michael and Saad said to Suham, when she'd scratched her arm against a piece of sharp metal piece hanging off of a kiosk.

She stood back and observed them work, tears circling her eyes. They were as rough with the luggage as Michael had been with Rita's heart.

They drove to Hannan's place, and while Michael waited in the taxi, Saad, accompanied by Suham, lifted the luggage, one at a time, to the third floor.

The young men loitering in the chicken booth with cigarettes in their mouths, the older gentlemen on the stairs with beads in their hands, and the children who stood beside their soccer balls or bikes, paused from their activities and watched the entire episode.

None of the men were home, just the ladies, which greatly relieved Suham. She didn't want to place Rita under more humiliating circumstances than this. Everyone greeted each other in a near whisper and with wretched expressions. Suham looked at Rita with pained eyes, but she could say nothing.

"Where would you like me to place the luggage?" Saad asked, after he'd dragged in the first one.

"Leave it where you are," Najat said. "That'll be fine."

But he moved it to the corner of the wall. "So no one will trip on it," he said.

After they'd done their duty, Saad and Suham excused themselves and left. Outside, Suham noticed that one of the spectators who'd watched them bring the luggage into the building was Rita's uncle. His eyes were red and squinted.

"Hurry up," Saad said behind her, while she was looking at the uncle's tormented face.

She entered the taxicab and felt terribly ill. She rolled down the window, and facing the wind, she allowed her tears to pour.

Suham wondered if Saad was taking them to his friend's house to compensate for the sorrow she'd been through in the last few days. It was a ludicrous concept, for her, of course, not for Michael. He seemed to enjoy wallowing in guilt as much as he did nonalcoholic beverages. He needed a rosary, she thought, to dangle through his throat until it touched his heart, to soak there a while, like the cabbage, cauliflower and carrot in her pickle jars, so it'd absorb all evil.

To Suham's surprise, the neighborhood they visited had various noises, spirited children, many walkers, and brilliant lights. It was as colorful as the portrait of Florence, Italy, she'd once seen on the cover of a travel magazine while grocery shopping, and it impressed her.

"Because of the cheap housing," Saad informed her, "most of the Chaldean refugees live here."

"Cheap housing, for this lively city?" Suham asked. "Isn't that a treat?"

"Not to Iraqis. They're used to three-story houses."

They climbed a hill that was nearly as straight as the skewers she barbecued shish kebabs on back in Stony Creek Park. They held each other's hands and jackets, so no one would fall over. When they arrived at the old building, which had no entrance door, Suham caught ten pairs of eyes staring down at her, from ten different windows.

They went up the stairs as cautiously as a bride walking down the aisle in a big dress. The railing inside the building was so weak that it swayed like a drunken man, and the smell of heavy spices floating about the air had a tranquilizing effect.

Saad knocked on the door.

"*Habbibi, iyouni, galbi...itfathel!*" The short chunky woman who opened the door honored Saad as though he was a prospective husband for her daughter.

She invited them into a room with brown carpeting, a yellow chipped ceiling, and a wall-size painting of a blue beach, a sun, and palm trees.

Michael smiled. "There are more people in here than there were in the street."

"Five families live here," Saad explained.

Everyone's conversation paused as Suham and Michael were seated on a fragile couch and were served hot cardamom tea and chocolate morsels. Then the noise of the television programs, of people talking and laughing, and of the doorbell ringing every ten minutes resumed. The instant a guest stepped into the house, he too was served tea and chocolate. It was like a bed-and-breakfast lodging.

Because so many people, of all ages, walked in and out of this room, Suham wouldn't have minded spending the rest of the night in their company, which was warmer than roasted chestnuts and more delightful than a good book. But one couple in particular had her immensely amused.

The wife tightened her jaws and shook her head every time Saleema's husband, Faysal, made blasphemous jokes, and furthermore, she accused him of being a sinner.

Faysal grinned while watching this woman squirm at his words. "Dear lady, I assure you I am not sinning," he said. "But you, by calling me a sinner, are!"

"If I am sinning, it's not because I have called you a sinner, but because I'm allowing myself to listen to you sin."

Each guest had their own way of covering their laughter, some with their hands and others with their teeth, as this woman, using verses from the Bible, continued to condemn Faysal, while her husband sat like a side dish next to the main course.

Her disapproval prompted Faysal to narrate a perverse joke about the Virgin Mary and Saddam Hussein's son, Oudai. "Saddam's son, Oudai, is killed so the next day, Saddam calls Heaven and the Virgin Mary answers, `Allou,` the Virgin Mary speaking.' Saddam asks, `Did my son make it to Heaven yet?' `No. Call back tomorrow.' Saddam calls the next day. `*Allou,* the Virgin Mary speaking.' `Has my son, Oudai, made it to Heaven yet?' `No, try back tomorrow.' The next day Saddam calls again. `*Allou,* Mary speaking.' `Hey, what happened to the Virgin Mary?' `Virgin? Oudai arrived last night. My God, do you think there are any virgins left up here?'"

After he'd given the punch line and everyone laughed whole-heartily, the woman pursed her lips and wiggled in her seat, intensifying her discomfort. "I ought to leave this house. I'm not supposed to hear such profanity."

"No, stay where you are, dear lady," Faysal begged.

"I must tell you a story then," the woman said. "Once I prayed so hard, I saw the Virgin Mary's face on my bedroom wall. I asked her for a child and the following week, I was pregnant."

The smiles on everyone's faces faded, but Suham knew no one's opinions of this woman's Godliness changed. Defending God's name because He gave her a child was one thing, but thinking she was better than the rest because she supposedly saw the Virgin Mary was another.

"I had specifically asked for this child to be born a girl," she stressed. "Because conditions in Iraq are not safe. A boy in war has to kill, and killing is a sin."

Everyone looked dumbfounded.

"And the great Virgin Mary gave me a girl."

"What the fuck!" Michael mumbled to Saad. "This lady is a beast!"

"Shhh," Suham hushed him, tapping him on the leg.

Shortly after the debate about religion, Michael and Suham excused themselves to leave, because the center table was set with shish kebab, rotisserie chicken, salad, olives and pickles. "I will let you get away today," Saleema said. "But only if you promise to come for dinner tomorrow."

Suham first said "No" but after much persuasion, and seeing how entertaining this house could be, she accepted the invitation, kissed Saleema on both cheeks and thanked her for her hospitality.

By the following night, a friendship had been established between Saad's cousins and his friends. They spent many nights eating, laughing, and drinking tea and Turkish coffee at each other's homes. Once Michael even invited two of the five families to Saad's work place, a fancy restaurant in the city of Jerush. The establishment was set half outside, half inside, and had a garden, a cave, a waterfall, a duck, two wild chickens, and a goat.

That day they had to take a taxi to the bus stop, a bus to Jerush, and a taxi to the restaurant, because being seven, they weren't able to bribe any one driver to take them all. On the way back, however, since it was dark and late, one man was courageous enough to risk taking all of them back to Amman in his taxi.

But not a minute after he drove off, a police officer followed him in a motorcycle.

"Pull over to the side and let me down," Michael said.

"Michael, no!" Suham said, at first worried.

"Pull on the side," he repeated to the driver.

The driver dropped Michael off at the corner of the street, and told him he'd pick him back up after he lost the cop. In the back seat, Suham and Saleema started laughing hysterically, as they waved goodbye to Michael. The driver went around in circles, waiting for the coast to clear, so Michael could sneak back into the cab.

Once they almost picked him up when Saleema shouted. "There's the police!"

He was hiding behind a store.

"Not yet! Not yet!" Everyone waved at Michael again, still laughing, as they passed him by. On the fifth spin, seeing that the police officer wasn't going to get off their tail, the driver shouted to Michael. "Go around this street and meet us where the big rocks are!"

The driver parked his car there, and waited for Michael to appear from the other side of the rocks. The women were laughing so hard that the men had to beg them to stay quiet so they wouldn't get caught. But they restrained themselves only seconds before they began chuckling again.

Michael finally came out from behind the big rocks, and rushed into the getaway car. "Go! Go!"

And for the next two hours, the time it took to get back to Amman, the women, tightly holding hands, laughed and cried in the back seat.

After this, Suham passed out the KOOL T-shirts, and gave away the cans of peanut butter, and the dozen pair of earrings to Saleema and whoever else lived in her house.

Chapter 20

❦

Early one morning, Suham asked their land-lord if he could send the maintenance man to the bakery for four loaves of bread, one meat pie and half dozen eggs. She had stopped cooking anything that required pots and pans, and only worked with the skillet.

She would have walked to the market herself, but for a while now the hot sun had been unbearable, and although she'd come to this country equipped with the "proper" clothing – which meant neither short nor sleeveless – people knew she was a tourist and stared at her anyway.

Suham sat on the couch and thought about her husband. She missed the way George called her from the store every night before he locked up to ask whether she'd run out of milk or juice, or if she was craving Tato Skins or Doritos.

"*Habbibi*, get me a can of Spam," she'd once surprised him. A sandwich of Spam, sliced tomatoes, and green peppers had been on her mind for a while.

Even if she was in the mood for elaborate foods, which meant making a stop at Ho-Wah restaurant or Beirut Palace, George did it without a single com-plaint. As complex as her desires got, however, her gratitude always remained simple; a smile, a gentle kiss and a "Thank you, *habbibi*".

Suham shifted in her seat, impatiently. If she could be beside her husband this second, she'd tell him a small secret; that his little efforts gave her enormous strength.

It wouldn't be long before she'd get that chance, though. Recently Michael had made plans that were larger than chateaus and stupider than wars, and Suham thought it best to go home now. He'd suggested, for instance, that they take a trip to Aqaba, a tourist region by the ocean, with Saleema and her husband. Suham had said "No", but that only made Michael argue harder.

The Egyptian maintenance man delivered the groceries; Suham covered the food's cost, handed him a tip, and started making breakfast. Michael had barely woken up and washed his face before he introduced the topic of Aqaba.

Suham had to explain, again, why she refused to go. "These people can't afford food much less four-day trips, Michael," she said, while scrambling four eggs with fried tomatoes. "You must stop telling them let's go here, let's go there."

"It doesn't really cost much, you know. Besides, Faysal has money stashed in his ceiling."

"He lives in an apartment!"

"But he still has a ceiling."

She turned off the stove and placed the pan of eggs and tomatoes on a rag in front of him. "It looks like Faysal is more of a devil than you are."

"I'm not sure about that," he said, dipping pita bread into the tomato juice. "I'd say he's a good man."

She served him a cup of tea, sat down across from him, and lit a cigarette. "He's a very good man, but he doesn't have a job."

"Neither do I!"

"Yes, and don't you find that weird?"

"Not technically."

She smoked her cigarette while observing him closely. He was as untouched by his break-up with Rita as a male dog was by its puppies. "I don't know why I bother, anyway. People with Iraqi passports can't go to Aqaba. They've caught a lot of them trying to swim across –"

"Never trust what the government says!" he interrupted. "They want to fool everyone. Old, young, gay, straight. Everyone. Even you, Aunt Suham."

She arched her brows, and shrugged one side of her shoulders. "Well, if you were capable of fooling me, why couldn't the government?"

He stopped chewing and his cheeks puffed out and his eyes grew bigger.

"Do not trouble yourself with looking confused," she said. "You pretended you came here to get married."

He swallowed and frowned at her. "I can't believe you're accusing me of lying."

"I am."

He frowned harder. "I wanted to go to Baghdad, damn it!"

"To have girls line up in church and for you to point your finger at the one who is most attractive?"

"Yeah!"

She rolled her eyes.

"If you think about it, you guys tricked me. You gave me only one choice. Only one! All my other friends, when they go to Baghdad, have as many girls to choose from as they do Chinese restaurants."

"And that impresses you?"

"Yeah."

She leaned back in her chair and smiled. "Then you want to go to Baghdad right now?"

He suddenly looked baffled. "I don't know."

This confirmed that it was time to go home. She stood up and pressed her cigarette into the astray. "I'm going to start packing. You're playing with this issue the way kids play with marbles."

She went into his room and studied his closet. A minute later, he appeared. "Can I start packing these colognes?" she asked, looking into the drawers and closet cupboards.

"Yeah."

She quickly took the colognes out. "Tell me what you'll wear at the airport."

"I don't know."

"You have to decide. Shorts or pants?"

"Pants, I guess. I don't know, maybe shorts. Keep one of each out."

She grabbed six of his shirts from the closet, settled them on the bottom of the luggage and flattened them. "You take everything to the cleaners the minute you get home, or else your mother will hand wash them, hang them to dry, iron them and then mop up the puddles they caused."

He nodded and she continued about her work.

"You didn't even need two suits to begin with," she went on. "Half of these clothes were not necessary. But when your mother and I counseled you, you got angry."

He kept quiet.

She hopped from room to room, with Michael behind her, because the third suitcase, which she planned on cramming with bottles, jars and liquids, lay in the kitchen. Holding the hair sprays and gel, she stopped and glanced at the wall. "Won't the bag weigh too much if I put all the perfumes and shampoos in it?"

He cleared his throat and twiddled his fingers around each other like old women with their rosaries. "I don't know –" he began. "I find Rita pretty most of the time, and then sometimes I wish she was tan or – can electrolysis take off all hair?"

She looked at him in utter amazement. "What hair are we talking about?"

"Just a little on her arms."

She sighed in relief. For a second there, she had suspected that Rita had been too willing and that had pushed Michael away. Then she realized the ludicrousness of what he'd just said.

"There is a farm in Rochester that raises genetically altered cows," she said. "It's only a couple of miles away from us. Why don't you see if they'll cook up a flawless bride for you?"

They were silent again for quite a while as she moved from room to room, cautiously coordinating the various articles of shoes, makeup, jewelry and towels in a fixed order, so that nothing could spill, leak, or break. Meanwhile, Michael remained frozen in place. His eyes explored the walls, the window, the floor, and the refrigerator, as though he found them as odd as she'd found the pizza her mother-in-law had introduced her to the night she arrived from Metro airport as a new bride.

"This is America's most famous dish," her mother-in-law had said, laughing at the awkward expression Suham made after tasting the pizza.

Suham had smiled, set the pizza back in her plate, and ate the stuffed onions and curried potatoes instead. This incident marked the start of Suham's worries because she realized then that she might not be able to fit into this civilization as easily as she'd thought.

"Should I call Rita?" Michael asked Suham, taking her by surprise.

She looked up from the luggage, with the shoes and perfumes in her hands, and she stood motionless in front of him. She had been praying night and day that he'd come to his senses and not return to Michigan empty handed, and until now, she'd thought her pleas had gone to waste.

She inhaled the happiness of this moment. "Why shouldn't you call her?"

He was very hesitant before he spoke. "Will she – accept my call?"

"She will, *habbibi*. She loves you."

Michael phoned the chicken booth and had the cook send a boy up to call Rita. When minutes later she picked up the receiver, Michael laughed. "How would you like to have dinner with my aunt?"

Whatever Rita said in return had Michael laughing, and after they talked for three or four minutes, he hung up.

"She said `yes'?" Suham asked.

"She said I was lucky to get a hold of her. She's moving into another apartment with her mom tomorrow."

They had dinner at the restaurant where Saad worked, since the occasion was too wonderful to celebrate it by eating eggs and meat pies indoors. Saad even got a few hours off to join his cousins for dinner.

Saad described to Suham his dreams and aspirations; once his brother sent him the three thousand dollars, he'd enter Greece unlawfully, reside there as a refugee, and while awaiting approval on the petition that the lawyer in Michigan was working on, he'd find a ninety hour a week job. "I'm going to save up the money my brother owes me before I even set foot inside America!"

"That's remarkable."

Sitting across from him, Suham listened to Michael insult the establishment they were eating in by comparing it to Cancun's Planet Hollywood, San Francisco's Hard-Rock Café, and Detroit's Renaissance Center.

"That's ridiculous," Suham mumbled. "It's like comparing China to India."

Sitting beside Michael, Rita melted whenever Michael fed her an olive or a cheese cube, and she applauded every word that came out of his mouth. "Even Baghdad has restaurants ten times as fancy as this."

Suham stared at the peach, apple and tangerine trees, the rows of grapevines, the bees hovering over the lilies and daisies, as she began to be as irritated by everyone's company as she was by Lisa's little intrusions.

The appetizers of *babba ghanouj, falafel, homous,* and small round *kubbas* made them request the cook to hold off an hour on their entrees, so they could leave the table and take a little walk. Michael and Rita took off in one direction, Suham and Saad in another.

"Hello Abu-Ahmad." Saad waved his hand to a man near the entrance gate who was weaving rugs. He turned to Suham. "Would you like him to make you one?"

"Oh no, no!" Suham replied, instantly.

He ignored her, though. "Tell me which colors you'd prefer."

"Please Saad, that's not necessary."

"What colors?"

She refused to name him the colors.

"Burgundy, purple and black," he told the man, anyway. "How long before it's ready?"

"Five to six days."

"Can't you have it for me sooner?"

"For you, *aghouya*, anything."

Saad walked beside her so haughtily, she felt like she'd been kissed without her consent.

"Let me show you why everyone comes to the small town of Jerush," he said, leading the way.

She did not want to be taken anywhere. She simply wished to return to their dinner table, but keeping in mind that Michael and Rita needed their privacy, she held her breath and continued her stroll beside Saad. He took her to the historical site above the restaurant grounds, helping her through a fence and holding her arm as she stepped over dirt and rocks.

He pointed out the areas where the queen and king sat when addressing their people and their castle. Then they walked between hundreds of thick tall poles, passing French and Japanese tour groups, and another with a heavy accented guide, English speaking.

On their way back, they stopped at tourist shops so Suham could buy her son a water pipe, her daughter a Jordanian costume, her sister a silver-plated teapot, and serving trays for her brothers' homes. While she and Saad bargained for some of the items, Saad offered to buy her a medallion.

"Absolutely not!" And she returned her attention to the merchant who wouldn't give her the costume for nine *dinars* apiece.

Saad must have taken her refusal as lightly as he would a joke because he came behind her and surprised her with a silver necklace that had green rhinestones. "To match your bracelet," he said, smiling.

"I'm sorry, Saad," she said, stupefied by the necklace. "I can't accept this."

And she pushed ahead of him. She badly wanted to be with her husband again.

He followed her, begging her to forgive him.

"I'm not upset, so there's nothing to forgive."

"I hope I didn't bother you in any way."

"No," she said, tightly, speeding back to the restaurant. "No more than you had when you told the entire Chaldean community that you were in love with me."

She'd half mumbled the words beneath her breath so he wouldn't go through extremes of defending himself to clear his name, change her opinion, gain her sympathy, and drain her self-disciplined manners. And she'd half said the words loud enough for him to hear, so he'd remember she was married, be a bit ashamed, and keep a distance.

She succeeded, she found out later during dinner. While eating shish kebab, drinking beer, and laughing at Michael's humor, Saad avoided her eyes as much as she had, many years back, avoided hearing from him the words "I love you".

Chapter 21

Rita was to sleep beside Suham that night, in the room with the queen-size bed. Because Rita had assumed she'd return home after dinner, she was without nightclothes so Suham loaned her pajamas. They closed the bedroom door, changed and perched over the bed quilts.

"Won't your family worry if you don't call?"

"They're clever," Rita said, smiling. "They'll know we've kissed and made up."

Suham grinned. "Have you kissed?"

Rita blushed and as she dropped her head, her hair veiled her face. She picked at the fabric of the quilt, with fingers that looked as soft as the pigeons Suham's father once brought home. Suham remembered rubbing their stomachs, while laying on the grass in her father's backyard, next to a radio playing Abid-Al Haleem Hafith, a famous Egyptian singer who was so loved that when he'd died at a young age, some girls jumped out of high-story buildings, killing themselves.

"Don't worry, I don't need a more elaborate answer," Suham said to stop Rita from taking shelter beneath the quilts. "I might forget I'm his aunt every now and then, but you won't."

There was a knock on the door, which lifted Rita's head up and brought back her natural paleness.

"*Itfathal*," Suham said.

Michael welcomed himself in, wearing his pajamas and grinning. He looked at them with delight and then laughed. "The two stooges!"

Suham smiled and rolled her eyes, and Rita turned to her with a confused expression. "What are stooges?"

Michael forced himself to look serious. "Didn't they teach you that word in school?"

"No, and I even had English tutors."

Michael laughed.

Rita blushed and turned to Suham. "What is a stooge?"

"It's what you, *habbibti*, will have to deal with all your life when you marry Michael."

Suham left them alone in the privacy they seemed to crave. She lay on the couch, watched television and waited Michael's exit so she could get into bed and sleep. But two hours passed, the lights turned off, and their voices died out. Suham realized she'd wasted too much time waiting and decided to sleep on the couch. She got a pillow and a blanket from the other room, turned off the television, and opened the windows so the cool breeze would take away her loneliness.

Her head faced the neighbors across the street, who at this late hour had a gathering of some sort. The curtains were drawn but their shadows played against them. The hostess, a large woman, served a tray of drinks, beginning from the left side of the room and moving clockwise.

She then placed the tray on the table and took her seat at the side, where the rest of the women were quietly clustered together, their hands fixed on their laps. The men's side, on the other hand, seemed to be having a heated discussion; their beads dangled like chandeliers as their arms worked and their bodies lifted an inch or two from the chairs.

It tortured Suham's heart, making her yearn to sleep in her sister's disordered guestroom, watch with curiosity the orange house at the end of Charleston Street. To gossip for hours on the phone. To attend numerous family functions, where she'd drink lots of cardamom tea. To tell her compliant daughter what to do. To make the laborious *tabbooleh*, *pacha*, and *kiliecha*. To avoid her neighbor Lisa's prying as well as her constant cheerfulness. To taunt her sister-in-law Alia and listen to her perverse interpretations of motives and actions.

She yearned to observe impishly George before he went to work, and to smile devilishly as he obeyed her every order.

The next morning, Suham woke up to the neighbor's children, two boys and a girl, fighting on their front porch about who had to go to the bakery for bread. Each made an excuse why they couldn't walk. One complained his toes hurt, the other his eyes, and the girl her stomach. The girl was exempt by default, because her whining was unbearable. "Dog, pig, deformed girl with cow's eyes!" the boys called her.

They threatened to twist her arms around her neck and stuff her into a sewage pipe once they came back from the bakery. As they sulked away, they kicked a rock, a tin can, and a fence in frustration.

Suham watched the girl closely as she played hopscotch. She seemed as affected by her brothers' threats as a greasy plate was by a drop of oil. Meanwhile, an older woman came out of the house and watered the driveway with a hose. When the boys came back with a paper bag, they swaggered up to the girl, as if they were gunslingers in a Mexican stand off. The girl's body was as firm as a bucket of apples as she waited.

"I'll mess your face with mud!" the taller boy said.

"I bet you'll get your hands dirtier than my face."

"I'll stuff your mouth with spider webs!" the shorter boy said.

"I bet they'll make you drool so much, you'll eat them instead." She rubbed her stomach and licked her lips. "Mmmm."

One boy pulled her braid, and she kicked his leg and sent him crying to the older woman. The woman said something to the boys, they said something to her that seemed to disturb her enough to drop the hose on the grass, walk to the side of the building and arch her neck. "Call your brother to come beat them," she yelled, and she went back to washing the driveway.

Suham looked in the direction the woman had yelled and the sight of a retarded boy startled her. He'd appeared behind the window out of thin air. Seconds later a young man came out of the house, had a word with the woman, then charged toward the two boys. When they saw him coming they ran the other direction and he chased after them, while the girl returned to playing hopscotch.

Rita came out of the bedroom and sat beside Suham on the couch. Her smile was shy, her cheeks rosy, and her eyes embarrassed. Suham knew Rita couldn't have given herself to Michael, but for an Arabic man, a lady lying naked beside him overnight could create enough doubts about her virtue to pull away from her. Especially since theirs was a formal and short acquaintance.

Rita flung her hair back and tilted her head sideways. "I've never met a man like Michael in all my life."

"Then you must send all the women who played any part in his life a letter of gratitude," Suham said. "Since men are often what women make them."

Rita's eyes turned away from Suham. "Am I acting like a school girl?"

"Don't mind me," Suham said, not having meant to fluster the poor girl. "I've been married for over twenty years."

Rita observed Suham with admiration. "Your husband worships you, doesn't he?"

Suham took a deep breath but did not answer. Instead, she diverted her attention to the neighbor's children, who were once again playing outside. She wondered if the boys had received a beating. She assumed not – there was no trace of sadness in their faces, there were ice cream cones in their hands.

"Does he, I mean your husband, understand you?"

"More than I give him credit for." Suham smiled sadly, realizing that for all these years his happiness hadn't revolved around her, but that he'd revolved himself around her happiness.

Rita was so much in love that she volunteered to make Michael's breakfast. "But I'll need your help," she said to Suham. "Tell me what he likes to eat in the morning, and how does he like it?"

"Eggs and tomatoes," Suham said. "It's the only thing we have in the refrigerator."

Suham taught Rita how to first slice the tomatoes into medium-size pieces, season them with salt and pepper, fry them in olive oil, until they'd lost most of their liquid, and then push them to one corner of the skillet to make room for the eggs; break the eggs into the skillet, without damaging their yolks, and place a lid over them. "Don't let the yolks harden, but don't serve it too soft either," Suham said.

Suham had tea on the couch, and allowed Rita to prepare the food with a single distraction. When Rita had finished setting the kitchen table with a cup of tea, bread, and a plate of the eggs and tomatoes, she asked Suham to come and applaud it.

Suham studied the table and had many criticisms; the tomatoes should have been fried longer, the egg yolk had hardened too much, the meal should've been left in the skillet, to better savor its juices; and, a woman must always serve the man a cup of tea after he sat down, not before, not only because the tea would be hottest then, but also because such a feminine gesture was warm, tender, and sensual.

But to save Rita from hurt feelings, Suham kept these criticisms to herself. When Michael came out of the room and saw the food, he said to Rita everything that had gone through Suham's mind, except for the enchanting business of serving tea. Of course, the way Michael spoke was so charming it impressed Rita instead of hurting her feelings.

They outlined their week's schedule. First they'd visit Shalalat Maein and swim in its pools. They'd spend half-a-day soaking their bodies in the Dead Sea's heavy salted water. They'd also see a few of Saad's friends in the town of Madaba. They'd take a tour to the historical land of Petra. Aqaba, however, they'd saved for Michael and Rita's honeymoon.

The next day, Suham and Rita wore their bathing suits underneath their clothes and left with Michael and Saad for Shalalat Maein. It was a long taxi ride, but the scenery of mountains and deserts, the humor of Michael's jokes and Saad's Baghdad stories made good company.

When they got there, however, they were all surprised at the size of the famous waterfall. "It looks like a little boy is urinating," Michael said, holding his stomach as he laughed.

Since the waterfall had disappointed them, Suham suggested they swim in the pools. Michael thought the idea absurd. "It's all men in there!"

"There's a smaller pool over there," she said, pointing to the opposite direction.

"Well, I still don't want to go," he said. "Swimming is for sissies."

"It's taken us hours to get here, and it'll take us hours to get back," she said tensely. "I'm going to make this place worth my while!"

She marched towards the swimming area before anyone had a chance to speak. She thought she was alone, when Saad caught up with her. He'd come to guard her against harassing men, as though he wasn't one of them. "Where did they go?" she asked about Michael and Rita.

"To a cafeteria, to drink beer and eat sandwiches."

In her shirt and skirt, Suham walked into a small pool occupied by women and children. She kept her clothes on like the other women, who swam with pants under their skirts and jackets over their shirts.

They'd left Shalalat Maein earlier than they'd expected, and they asked the taxi driver if he could take them some place interesting. "There's a zoo, just forty-five minutes away from here," he said with a big smile. Michael told him to drive them there.

They arrived at a big field, and the driver anxiously led them to what he called "the animals". The animals he'd boasted about were some twenty or thirty deer living in a wall-fenced ranch. To see them,

Suham, Rita, Michael and Saad took turns peering through a small barred window. It was as if they were visiting prisoners in the old-fashioned days.

"Take pictures," the driver said, pointing to Saad's camera. "Take pictures."

Saad stood as dumbfounded as everyone else, not able to comprehend what panorama the driver wanted them to seize – the wall or the barred window. Seeing that they were baffled by his dictation, the driver took the camera from Saad's hand and told them to huddle together.

"This guy is a complete moron," Michael mumbled, as he put one arm around Suham, another around Rita, and smiled at the camera.

The following day, they took a trip to the Dead Sea. They had the driver park in a secluded area where they wouldn't be disturbed by tourists and so the women could swim comfortably in their bathing suits. Still, because of the driver, whose eyes had kept returning to Suham and Rita in the rearview mirror, they decided to stay in their dresses.

There were nearly as many fish bones on the shore as there was sand. The water of the Dead Sea had so much salt it killed all living organisms. "Keep your head above water, or else it'll burn your eyes," everybody warned everybody else before they began wading.

It wasn't difficult to keep one's head above the water, though, since it cradled them like infants. As the sun beat down on their faces, Suham and Rita's dresses billowed out their waists and their bodies sailed in the water.

Suham closed her eyes and remembered the day of Michael's party when she'd snuck into Wadi's room before dinner was served to have a cigarette. The wind had moved the curtains then as the water now moved her. She wondered if it was possible to be as peaceful and carefree standing on dry land as it was lying in this sea.

When they got out, they drove on to a waterfall that people used as a douche to rinse off the salt their skin and clothes had absorbed. But they were stopped at the border by government officials, who, because of Saad and Rita's Iraqi passports, refused to permit them entrance. The taxi driver, Saad and Michael walked out of the car and pleaded with the officers to let them through for just fifteen minutes. "*Ya-Allah*, just so we can shower!" Michael said, pointing at his clothes.

"I cannot, *ya-aghouya*," one of the officers said. "It's against government regulations."

"But we have tourists from America that wish to see the other side," Saad said, stressing the word America, like it was the name of the Queen.

"*Aghouya*, this is Saddam's orders, not ours!" one of the officers said.

Seeing there was no use in arguing further, they drove to the more populated region of the Dead Sea, and took indoor showers instead. When it started getting late, they bought *shawarma* sandwiches, peaches, cucumbers, tomatoes and sodas and went home. They were so exhausted by the time they got there, they barely took a few bites of their food before they all, even Saad, fell asleep.

Chapter 22

The fact that Saad spent the night was not a problem, if Suham could avoid him in the morning before he set off for work. She suspected that, ever since she'd turned down the necklace, he'd stewed a dialogue in defense of his behavior. To thicken this stew with extra intensity and spice it up with more drama, he'd probably been rehearsing his monologue and was waiting for a suitable moment to recite it.

She tried to pretend she was sleeping when she heard him walk out of the bedroom, but her impatience got her into trouble. She opened her eyes for a split second and he caught her.

"Good morning," she said.

"Good morning."

She had no choice but to get up and be a good hostess. "Would you like some breakfast?"

"No, but if you can make me a cup of tea, I'd appreciate it."

She smoothed her nightgown from her thighs to her ankles before pushing away the covers and getting off the couch. "I can make you eggs," she said.

"Tea will be fine," he said and went into the bathroom.

She walked into the kitchen, filled the teakettle

and placed it on the stove.   While waiting for the water to boil, she sat on the couch and looked out the window.   The neighbors were still sound asleep. She imagined warm homes behind the windows, with children quarreling in the morning, lamb soup simmering in the afternoon, and husband and wife kissing at night; the kind of home hers was before Nisreen and Fadi moved out and Suham's tolerance for George shrunk considerably.   It had been much easier to acknowledge him as a good father than it was as a devoted husband.

The water faucet that had been running in the bathroom turned off and Suham held her breath.   Her cousin had probably stood in front of the mirror all this time to rehearse his speech yet one more time before the final performance.

He walked into the family room and sat on the couch across from her.   "If you don't mind, I'd like to have a word with you."

She wanted to stop him from spilling over the stew he'd been simmering for days, but his words had already dropped out of his mouth, like peas from a bowl.   She missed half his speech while trying to figure a way out of this discussion.

"— and because you are such a dear cousin to me, I don't want you to think, not even for a minute, not even a second, that my intentions were in any way, at any time, disrespectful."

The show deserved a standing ovation, even if she had skipped most of its performances.   He rubbed his eyebrows and resumed with elaborations that were as confusing to her as adverbs and predicates had been when her daughter Nisreen studied them in junior high school.   Suham saw that there was no sense in trying to interrupt him, so she went to the kitchen, put a few spoons of tea into the kettle, lit a cigarette and leaned against the counter, nodding and smoking as he went on and on and on.

When he was done, she served him his tea and kept standing. "Well, I'm glad your intentions were as innocent as you say they were, Saad," she said. "Because, although I don't mention his name often, I am very much in love with my husband."

His eyes twitched, as if he'd just been given a shot in the cheek. "And that is – how it should be," he stammered. He cleared his throat, patted his pants and stood up. "Well, I must go to work now."

And he left without drinking his tea.

Suham sighed. She blamed herself for putting her cousin in such an uncomfortable position. She should've, from the very beginning, given a high account of her husband.

In the afternoon, as Suham pealed garlic and Rita got out dried peppermint leaves for the cucumber stew they planned on cooking for dinner, the telephone rang. It startled them both. Rita's hand on her chest, she burst into laughter. "That nearly stopped my heart!"

Suham prayed it wouldn't be Saad calling, because if it was, she would have to be as mean with him as she was with the Chaldean women who, on one or two occasions, had passed her by without exchanging greetings. When she had later, to their surprise, confronted them, they'd alleged they hadn't seen her at so and so's party or at that particular mall.

Rita set the jar of peppermint down and answered the telephone. She greeted the person on the other end of the line smilingly, said "yes" and "no" several times, and then hung up the phone gravely.

"My uncle and my cousin's husband are coming here," Rita said. "They want to talk to Michael."

Suham put down the garlic bulb on the table, and she folded her arms beneath her chest. "Are they bringing their rifles?"

"They don't trust Michael."

"That's understandable," Suham said. "At this point, I don't trust him myself."

"They don't trust me, either."

"Why should they, *habbibti*?" Suham said, laughing. "You've refused dozens of perfectly legitimate suitors to chase a man as inconsistent as Michael."

Rita grinned and looked away, evidently enjoying the label of having been a heartbreaker, a role Suham had mastered at the early age of fourteen, and had been as recently involved in it as this morning.

Suham wiped the garlic skin off the table and then she twisted the lid over the peppermint leaves jar. "We have to clean up," she said. "Check and see if we have enough coffee in the cupboards."

"We do."

Suham paused and looked around her. "Then I guess we just need to clean up."

While Suham threw dishes and utensils into the sink, Rita approached her, timidly. "Do you think this is bad timing?"

"Not one bit," Suham said. "If anything, this will benefit you."

Suham worried that if given a few more nights of her lenient chaperoning, Rita would completely surrender herself to Michael.

"I've been so busy with Michael's mood swings," Suham continued, "I've forgotten that your family exists. It's as though this wedding is centered around a groom and nothing else."

"Yes, but won't this frighten Michael?"

In deep contemplation, Suham gazed out the window. She wanted to protect Rita's honor, but at the same time, she didn't want Michael to start having doubts again. "I don't know, Rita. I can't tell with Michael anymore."

Rita bent her head.

"If it'll make you feel any better, know that it's not up to us to alter the situation to Michael's advantage," Suham said. "Your family will not stand for it."

Standing firm, Rita took in a deep breath, and then nodded her head in understanding.

In the beginning of their visit, the men talked about the weather. The city of Amman, having a reputation for being mildly warm, was hotter than they'd expected during the month of June. Its high temperatures had even surprised its natives.

Suham carried a tray of Turkish coffee from the kitchen to serve her guests. Rita followed, offering individually wrapped chocolates she'd poured into a crystal bowl. "I guess Baghdad's heat is rubbing off on it," Suham said.

"Perhaps," Hannan's husband, Kussay, said. "I doubt, though, it'll ever be as hot as Baghdad's sun is in June."

"No, of course not." Before taking their seats, Suham returned the empty tray to the kitchen and Rita placed the bowl of chocolates on the table.

When the subject of weather was dropped, the men took up the issue of Kussay's refugee status. He and his family had filed a petition that might allow them entrance into New Zealand.

"I thought you were going to Australia," Suham said with surprise.

"But you see, nowadays, Australia is almost as hard to get into as America."

Suham was in a daze. She'd found Michigan difficult to live in, despite its population of some one million Middle Easterners, so she marveled at how this family planned to survive in a country with no Arab residents. "New Zealand is an extraordinary route."

"Yes, it is far," he said, not comprehending her well. "It isn't an easy route, either. You see, we need to first qualify, by points. Each one of our characteristics gets a score."

Suham frowned in confusion.

"Say if I'm single, I get five points," he said, seeing her expression. "If I have a college degree, I get another ten. If they add up to a high enough number, we're permitted entry."

Suham was fascinated with this information as she had been to the sight of young boys and girls kissing in public malls and restaurants when she'd first come to America. But it saddened her to hear such things; the more people fled from Iraq, the more rules other countries set up against them. Despite her interest in these facts, however, she stopped making inquires and gave brief answers to their questions, because she wanted the men to get down to what they originally came here to say.

Finally there came a moment of utter stillness, after which Rita's uncle cleared his throat and gave a sermon. "I have my bus ticket right here." His eyes on Michael, he slipped his hands in his pant pocket and brought out a folded paper. "I'm to leave for Baghdad Friday. I bought it thinking things were over between you and Rita."

Everyone bent their heads, like the Chaldean people did Sunday Mass when the usher rang the bell and the priest showered the first three or four rows with incense.

"I need to go back to my work – " He paused and looked at Rita with such tender eyes it pained Suham to witness it.

He then turned to Michael. "When her father passed away, I treated Rita better than I did my daughters. The thought of her going to America tore my heart to pieces –"

He pressed his fingers against his watering eyes. "But I said to myself, *aghouya*, what's more important, Rita's happiness or your emptiness? The answer was simple. Of course, Rita's happiness, because in the long run, this precious girl's happiness will wipe out all my emptiness."

His eyes shone like wet marbles, and the tears started swimming back up his lashes. He had to quit talking and his son-in-law took over. His sermon was professional and colder, but it was honest.

"You are intelligent people. You are good-hearted people. That is why we are trying to be patient and understanding under these unusual circumstances. Had you been any other family, we would not have tolerated this form of engagement."

Kussay looked towards Rita, then to the uncle, then to Michael. "Rita thinks highly of you and your aunt," he said. "And so do we."

Suham thought it time to return their courtesy, since Michael was avoiding this discussion so determinedly. "I thank you for your kind words," she said. "And if you are accommodating your principles for our sake, it is because you know that we, sincerely, honor your family even more than you do ours."

Kussay thanked her while nodding his head.

The uncle, having recollected himself, inclined slightly forward in Michael's direction. "My ultimate joy would be to see Rita get married before I leave, if that's anywhere in your plans. I'm leaving Friday. I'm leaving after tomorrow."

Everyone bent their heads again.

He raised his ticket a few inches in the air. "I can

extend the date, if only I hear him utter the words..."

Michael did not make a sound, or move a muscle. Suham was more irritated by his stillness than she'd ever been by George or anyone else she'd ever encountered.

"Is there something that Michael isn't telling us?" Kussay asked with hesitation. "I mean, is the problem Rita, or is it family pressure? Or is there – is there something awaiting him in America?"

"No, nothing like that!" Suham jumped, damning Michael for his selfishness. He was smudging the family name because now Rita's side either assumed he had an unfit lover in Michigan or children out of wedlock.

The room was quiet, as though no one believed her. She didn't know what more to say, because to further defend Michael's name would convince them that she was lying.

"Well, there is no refund on this bus ticket," the uncle said. "But if your plans are pure – if they're settled – I'll go down to the station this minute and change my departure."

The room was quiet.

"What do you say, Michael?" the uncle persisted, with a kind smile. "Will I get to see my niece's wedding?"

"*Inshallah.*"

God willing. Once those words were articulated from Michael's lips, the remainder of this visit centered around setting a wedding date. The families agreed on Friday. "Then I will leave for Baghdad Saturday," the uncle said.

The men then took their leave, with lots of happiness in their eyes and laughter in their voices.

Chapter 23

Once her company left, Suham cleared the table of coffee cups and green, purple, and yellow chocolate wrappers. She then telephoned the land-lord and complained about the bathroom facilities not working properly. He promised he'd send the plumber to fix it. "We have to leave soon, so if it takes more than ten minutes for someone to come up here," she threatened, "I'll be very upset."

"*La, la, ya-ughti, la tighafien,*" he pledged. "I'll cut off my right arm before I'll let you get upset."

Suham hung up the phone and wiped the coun-ters, washed the dishes, and canceled the cucumber stew they'd intended to cook earlier. She proposed they eat out instead.

"Only if it's at Saad's restaurant," Michael said as he walked into the bathroom and closed the door behind him.

Suham wrapped the peeled garlic in plastic and placed them in the refrigerator next to the cucumbers. She washed her hands diligently, to dissolve the garlic smell as well as any dirt, and she went into the bed-room to pick out what she was going to wear.

"Michael's been in the bathroom for forty minutes," Rita complained later, holding a towel under the kitchen faucet, to let the water soak it. "And I don't know why."

Suham smiled. "Do you want me to solve the puzzle?"

Rita pressed the wet towel against her face, removed it, then folded it slowly, as though it was made out of silk instead of cotton. "Maybe he's too frightened to come out and live up to his word," she said, reluctantly.

"Oh, don't be so scared!" Suham lifted Rita's chin up with her hand so their eyes met. "Because if you are, you'll make it easier for him to act like a jerk."

Michael wouldn't have come out of the bathroom had the plumber not arrived. As he went into the kitchen, he ignored Rita and Suham, as though they were shadows. His behavior intimidated the ladies, so when they exchanged words to each other, they whispered.

They left the apartment. Outside, the landlord came out of his office and asked Suham if he'd had the honor of gaining her approval today.

"Yes, thank you."

"Take this advise from me," the landlord addressed Michael. "Don't ever try to break your aunt's word."

"This one here?" Suham laughed with sarcasm. "Why, for the past few weeks, he's been breaking my words as fast as he breaks walnuts."

The landlord smiled. "And what punishment have you in store for him, madam?"

Suham sighed, heavily. "I'm afraid this time, my nephew will have to lay out his own punishment."

At the restaurant, they informed Saad of what had taken place earlier in the afternoon; how Rita's uncle and her cousin's husband paid them a visit, which had prompted a wedding date. Starting with the left and turning clockwise, Saad passed out some twenty words of congratulations to each person.

"I know an excellent baker for buying the cake," he offered. "And a very decent jeweler for the gold bands. Faysal has a keyboard organ, and I have a friend who owns a video camera."

Suham was truly grateful that Saad could help her minister the wedding, only two days away. "See if you can take tomorrow and Friday off from work."

He agreed, and they decided to meet at Saleema's place early the following morning.

"You're blowing this whole thing out of proportion," Michael said in the taxi on their way back home. As casual as he tried to be about his comment, he couldn't hide his meanness.

"I wasn't expecting to reserve horse carriages and hire trumpeters." Suham turned to Rita. "Were you?"

Rita lowered her head. "No."

"We don't need anything but a priest. And even that, I can do without," he said, aggravated. "I don't trust them with my money, and I'm not about to trust them with my marriage license."

No one said a word.

"I mean, why the hurry?" he said out loud. "You guys act like by tomorrow, the jewelry store will be robbed and the bakery will run out of batter and we'll be doomed!"

"Michael, *habbibi* –"

"Wedding bands!" he interrupted, and she knew nothing she could say would stop him now. "Wedding cake! Next thing you know you'll be suggesting wedding invitations!"

His temper worried Suham, so she softened her heart quicker than a flame did cold wax. "I didn't mean to hurry things, Michael. I was just talking."

"You guys keep pumping the wedding up, and I have more fucking pressure on me than a hooker doing five guys at one time."

Before he went more out of control, she became even calmer and repeated, "I was just talking, Michael. I didn't mean to upset you. I'm sorry."

He started mumbling a lot of things about what was right and wrong in life. "Never involve the family in your business! Never! I made that mistake this time, but never again!"

He'd turned so mean, Suham didn't recognize him. For a split second, she felt like they'd been hijacked by a hitchhiker the driver had just picked up off the road. He was talking to her as disrespectfully as she'd seen him do with his mother. "If planning the wedding is putting too much pressure on you," she broke in, somewhere in his rating about everyone's mentality, "then I'll remove myself from it entirely."

For the remainder of the ride, Michael glared ahead and Suham kept quiet and simply stared out the window, something Rita had been smart enough to do from the very beginning. She watched the sky and prayed that Michael's anger wouldn't ruin things between him and Rita, if they weren't already.

Rita came to Suham in the middle of the night and sat on the edge of the couch. Her presence hadn't startled Suham, because she wasn't asleep, either.

It took Rita a while to express what troubled her. "I don't want Michael to wake up the day after our wedding and regret what he's done."

Suham sighed and she too took a while before replying. "If you suspect he might do that, would you still marry him?"

Rita tilted her eyes down. "I love him."

The stillness of the room carried a weight beyond description. "Then, *habbibti*, I cannot help you."

Saleema wasn't at home when they arrived at her apartment the next morning. Two girls and a man who belonged to the other families told them Saleema had gone grocery shopping and would be back in an hour. "But please come in for coffee, anyway," they said.

Shortly after, the man took Michael back out again, to introduce him to some of his friends.

"Would you mind keeping me company while I make the coffee?" the younger girl asked Rita.

"Of course not." And Rita followed the girl into the kitchen.

"I hate my sister," the older girl immediately revealed to Suham, startling her. "She's the most wicked girl I've met. She made Saleema so mad yesterday that her yelling was louder than the Mosque's evening prayer."

The girl glanced towards the kitchen, brought herself closer to Suham and whispered. "What's going on with your nephew and her?"

"They're getting married tomorrow."

"Oh, wonderful!" she screeched, her palm on her chest. "God bless them both! May they have the healthiest children, see the happiest days, live the longest lives!"

"Thank you, *youm al-ilich*," Suham wished the same for the girl.

"My sister is the biggest whore," the girl said, returning to her sitting position and no longer whispering. "Her boyfriend bought her a gold bracelet and she cheats on him. With two guys."

Suham wondered how that was possible, since her sister had a jaw as prominent as the hill that led to this building and a nose as layered and compacted as a cauliflower.

This gripping conversation was disrupted by the other sister coming out of the kitchen with a tray of Turkish coffee, followed by Rita. They drank coffee, and later tea, and much later, Michael returned.

Michael was a different man than the one in the taxi the night before. Since Saad hadn't been able to leave his work, he'd told Michael what to do, who to call, and where to go. On his own, Michael used these instructions to put together the wedding reception. He ordered a heart-shaped cake, he included a dinner menu and liquor, he rented light bulbs with long cords, he reserved Saad's friend's video camera, and he asked Faysal to find a drummer and a guitarist who'd team up with his organ. "Then we'll have a whole band," Michael said.

Suham and Rita looked at each other and smiled as they watched Michael's designs multiply. He assigned everyone in the room a task; one was to pick up the cake, one to pay the restaurant a deposit, one to telephone the cameraman, one to help Faysal move the musical instruments.

They discussed where they ought to have the reception. Saleema offered her home, but since Michael had invited the five families and their friends, and whomever else he'd acquainted himself with while making the wedding reservations, it was voted out as being too small.

Faysal proposed they have it on the building's roof. "I'm sure the landlord won't mind," he said. "I'll talk to him first thing tomorrow morning."

This idea was applauded.

Saleema said she once worked at a salon. "I can

do your hair," she said to Suham and Rita, "as long as you have a hair dryer and hair spray."

Suham and Rita impatiently awaited Saad's arrival. To prepare the marriage license, they still had to see the priest who'd perform the wedding ceremony tomorrow. Because Saad was the best man, he had to be a witness. Suham asked the older girl who'd talked so badly about her sister earlier if she could be Rita's maid-of-honor, since she herself, being a married woman, couldn't take on that role.

"I don't have a decent dress!" the girl cried.

"I'll lend you one of mine." The girl's figure was larger than Rita's but smaller than Suham's. Tightening the belt a notch or two would do the trick.

Suham suddenly turned to Rita. "You haven't tried on the dress I've gotten you!"

"Oh." Rita frowned, as if she'd forgotten all about it too.

Suham believed she was pretending, though. Rita and Nisreen were approximately the same size and Suham had brought Nisreen's long sequined white evening dress and the veil she'd married in for Rita to wear. Like all other Chaldeans who selected their brides from Baghdad, Michael planned on buying Rita a real wedding gown and her own veil in Michigan, where the fancy wedding would be held.

Suham had only mentioned the dress over the phone while she was still in America and Rita might have been under the impression that it was never delivered.

"Don't worry, it'll fit. Your measurements are so close, you'll be borrowing clothes from each other in America." Suham smiled tenderly as she observed Rita. "You'll be like sisters."

Saad arrived after dark. He held a black suit on a hanger over his shoulders, and seeing everyone was as anxious to leave as animals were to eat, he stood still. "Please, I must get a bite to eat first."

Saleema made him a cheese, tomato and cucumber sandwich and handed it to him as he was shoved out the door by Suham, Michael, Rita and the maid-of-honor.

"Do you have flowers I can put in my hair tomorrow?" the girl asked Suham.

"No."

"A ribbon?"

Suham looked at her and imagined how ridiculous she'd be with any accessories, since her face in the midst of her fluffy hair was as small as a cherry on top of a whole pie. Decorating herself with ribbons and flowers would be like trimming the cherry with whip cream.

A nun had them wait in a cozy office until the priest presented himself. He took his seat behind the desk, and asked for the fiancé and his fiancée's birth certificates, single hood papers that were stamped with their hometown priest's approval, and their passports. He asked Michael and Rita a dozen questions, filled out some forms, which they'd have to sign the next day, gave a little lecture about the holy definition of matrimony, and asked who their parents were.

After giving their ancestors' names, the priest went into deep meditation. Then he nodded his head. "I knew your father," he said to Michael. And he explained how he and Michael's father, before he'd married and moved to Baghdad, had lived in the village of Telkaif. "I knew your mother too. Tell her Father Ayoub – she'll remember."

After they chatted for fifteen minutes, the priest got to his feet, shook their hands and told them to be in church the next day at six o'clock in the evening.

They returned to Saleema's house to drop the girl

off. "I'm sorry, what is your name?" Michael asked while they climbed the hill. "I keep forgetting."

"Haifa."

Suham and Rita looked at each other and giggled. Michael asked them what was the matter. "Couldn't you have asked me for her name?" Suham asked.

"I didn't think you'd know it."

When they entered the apartment, Suham was blinded by the sight of some ten people walking around in black T-shirts with the word KOOL in florescent green letters printed on their chests. Suham would've burst into laughter had not Michael smiled, devilishly. "What the fuck!"

"Hush!" she whispered, while slapping his arm. She was relieved, though. Having stopped him from mocking this scene hindered her laughter.

In their KOOL T-shirts, the people celebrated Michael's and Rita's forthcoming union with lots of cardamom tea and solid chocolates.

"I know you!" Faysal said to Rita, with bewildered eyes, alarming everyone. Then he asked if she was from so and so family and was the daughter of so and so sergeant.

"Yes."

His eyes grew larger, as if he'd just discovered the long gone Um-Kalthoum was having tea in his living room. "How were you able to part with your fortune?"

With a gentle smile, Rita bent her eyes, while he continued to look amazed. "She was living like royalty in Baghdad," he said to everyone, then turned to her again. "Weren't you?"

She remained silent.

"Royalty or not, who'd want to stay in Baghdad," his wife muttered.

"I love it there," Rita said.

"Love what about it, *habbibti*, that it has no water, no milk, no eggs, no meat, no sugar," Saleema said, bitterly. "That if you want the cake your fiancé just ordered, you have to buy it from the black market."

"No water, no eggs, no meat?" Rita laughed. "That is absolutely not true!"

The men respectfully disagreed with Rita's statement, and they all testified to Iraq having such a serious food and medicine shortage that out of desperation, its people turned to theft and crime. "Did your eyes not see merchants in the streets selling a tablespoon of tomato paste in a plastic bag?" Saleema asked with hostility. "Did your eyes not see people drink water with worms and dirt swimming in it?"

The room became silent.

Rita realized she'd either been insensitive to these people's hardships, or ignorant of Iraq's dreadful conditions, because she changed her opinion. "I suppose there was such despair," she said, "but I had been unaware of it."

The subject ended at that point, but the steam coming out of Saleema's nose continued to rise, making her look like a teakettle with two beaks.

On their way home, in the back seat of the taxi, Rita rested her head on Michael's chest while he put his arm around her. He kissed her cheek on a few occasions, stroked her stomach once, and teased her about not having good taste in music, since she wasn't as crazy about the Iraqi singer Kathim Al-Sahir, whom he said was "the man voted #1 in all the Middle East!" as she was about Najwa Karem, a young Lebanese singer, whom he said was "popular but no genius."

Suham sighed with weariness. The work she'd put into this wedding was finally paying off. Now she ached to be home, on Charleston Street.

They arrived at the apartment exhausted and they scattered, the way black pepper did when it landed in a cup of water, to find their beds. A strange feeling crept over Suham. More than all the other nights, she thought it unwise for Rita to share a bed with Michael, since his mood had wavered too often in the past twenty-four hours.

If it was up to her, she'd knock on their door and give Rita a suggestion or two. "Oh, Rita, *habbibti*," she'd start off saying, for instance, in a casual manner, to prevent her feelings from getting hurt, "Michael might have nightmares of his whores grouped together in mourning, wearing black dresses and holding Kleenexes to their nose. And since consequently, he'll wake up drenched in sweat and he'll cancel the wedding, why don't you play it safe and kick him out of your bed?"

But thank God, it was no longer up to her.

Chapter 24

❧

The very first drop of noise that spilt into Suham's consciousness was Rita's voice. It felt like an okra's prickly stem, which was neither painful nor nice. Suham would have judged the voice's substance a lot better had she been entirely awake. Her eyes remained closed, as though they had on them *amar el-deen*, moon of the religion, a sticky sheet of candy made with a sweetened dried apricot puree.

She heard the voice again, louder this time. As she started to drift away from her dreams and realize the content of Rita's words, she aimed to switch this morning into last night, the way she used to do with certain leftover meals. For instance, if she cooked a pot of stuffed zucchini one day and her family did not finish it, the following day, she'd make a roast, and hide it in the oven, where no one usually checked, since her food was most often left on top of the stove. She'd reheat the pot of stuffed zucchini and serve it to her family for the earlier part of the day, then when it was consumed, she'd make the roast appear like magic, for dinner.

Again she heard Rita's voice. Suham wanted to walk to the kitchen and plug her ears with a handful of rice, but feeling too drained to get off the couch, she found an alternative: concentrating on the neighbor's children who quarreled outside. Their soccer ball had fallen beneath a parked vehicle, and each one of them refused to wiggle their bodies between the road and the muffler to retrieve it.

She removed the *amar el-deen* from over her eyes and was taken aback by the bright and sunny morning. Under the circumstances, she'd expected it to be gloomy and dark. But it wasn't. Perhaps the news hadn't reached God yet.

Michael came out of the bedroom and sat on the couch opposite hers. He ducked his head into the palm of his hands, like a cat into a bowl of milk. Suham wanted to kindly pet her nephew until his fear rose from his stomach and through his throat.

Rita then came out of the bedroom. She'd powdered her cheeks with a few tears. "Your nephew had his way."

Suham was as unstirred by this comment as *dolemma* was by its cook. The stuffed vegetables in this dish were packed tightly together so they wouldn't fall apart while the steam danced amongst them. Starting from the bottom up, the frame inside the pot looked like this: a layer of stuffed cabbage leaves, then of stuffed eggplants, zucchini, cucumbers, green peppers, tomatoes, then of stuffed onions, and finally at the very top of the tower, stuffed grape leaves. Once *dolemma* was cooked, with a little bit of water and lemon juice, a woman used all her might to safely flip the pot over onto a tray, the way a huge heavy cake would have to be.

Rita wiped the left side of her face with trembling hands. "I'm going home."

Only then did Suham notice Rita holding a jacket in her arms and a purse over her shoulder. Michael's head remained in the bowl of milk and Suham stayed as unstirred as *dolemma.*

Then Rita disappeared.

Suham stared out at the neighbors, but this time she was in such distress she could barely see or hear the children. "I can't look at you, Michael," she muttered, "so you must leave me alone."

She'd meant for him to stand up and walk away. But he surrendered his seat no better than he did his single hood.

"Then I shall leave." Suham got off the couch and went knocking on Saad's bedroom door.

Saad came out with a bare chest and a puzzled facial expression. "What's the matter?"

"Rita left," she said, as simply as she would have said good morning. "Michael has changed his mind again."

Saad hopped into the family room to rescue Michael, as Suham made a pot of fresh tea. She heard him light a cigarette and smoke, and she waited for him to initiate the talk. When she saw that he was as lost for words as Michael was for common sense, she approached them both. "Are you on his side?"

Saad looked at her with frightened eyes. "No!"

"Then advice should be coming out of your mouth, not cigarette smoke!"

She stood solidly in front of him as he flattened the cigarette in the astray. Giving both men a harsh stare, she turned around and marched to the kitchen.

There was a knock on the door. It was Faysal and his gentlemen friends. "Saleema said that if you want her to get your hair done on time, you have to wash it now, because she'll be here by..."

He stopped talking as Suham's eyes fell to the ground.

"What's the matter?"

"I don't know," she mumbled and then made room for him and his friends to come in.

The men greeted each other formally, aware of a problem lurking in the air. To lighten up the atmosphere, they teased and joked with Michael. They bullied him. They shared their experiences with him.

"Michael, *habbibi*," one of the guys said. "I'd kneel down and kiss the ground a thousand times if I was lucky enough to have a girl as beautiful and as intelligent as Rita."

"*Yalla aghouya*," another man said. "A gigantic cake is on its way to Faysal's house, and as you told us to do, we've given the restaurant owner the deposit for the food."

One of the guys rubbed Faysal's belly, making it bounce up and down. "If we don't have a wedding tonight, we'll have a corpse! Faysel won't let a crumb go to waste."

"*Wallah, Wallah!*" someone swore to God. "With or without a groom, I'm eating kebabs and onions and chicken and beets and cake at Faysal's tonight!"

"And beer!" someone else reminded him.

"And beer!" The man raised his hand as if to show off a trophy.

The men laughed, but they hadn't influenced Michael's mood a bit. He kept saying, "I can't. I'm confused".

When the men discovered how sturdy his decision was, they were as alarmed by Michael's behavior today as she had been every day of this trip. And like her, when she'd first seen this side of Michael, they continued trying to make him think differently.

Suham leaned against the refrigerator and she prayed. She made an oath that, if today's wedding proceeded somehow, she'd live on nothing but bread and water, fruits and vegetables for forty days. Furthermore, she'd never, unless in an emergency, leave George home alone overnight; not once a week, not once a month, not once a year. Also, she'd attend church every Sunday and throw five dollars in the basket at each visit.

The doorbell rang again. When Suham answered it, the sight of Saleema's wicked smile irked her. She must know. One of Suham's guests must have left to broadcast the news. Saleema kissed Suham on both cheeks and entered the apartment, as jolly as a young girl who'd just made her boyfriend jealous.

"I told Faysal yesterday," Saleema said, sitting down and fixing her purse on her lap. "I told him this wasn't going to work out."

Outraged, Suham didn't know how she was going to keep her composure and not charge at Saleema with insults.

"I could tell last night you didn't want her," Saleema addressed Michael, "just by the way you had your hands on your legs while she leaned towards you."

Michael had barely spoken to the men, but now he regained his energy, as though Saleema was fuel for his empty gasoline tank. "I'm not ready. I want to take my time, that's all."

"But *aghouya*, with no disrespect to your opinion," Faysal said, "didn't you think about that before you asked the girl to meet you in Jordan?"

"Yes, but we had an agreement. If I saw her and it didn't work out, we'd go our own separate ways."

Faysal arched his brows. "But there's nothing wrong with her."

"There doesn't have to be something wrong with her. Maybe she's perfect for someone else, not me."

Looking astounded, Faysal laughed sarcastically. "*Aghouya, azzizi*, if you ask me, I think you're doing this out of stubbornness..."

"Stubbornness?" Michael interrupted. "Not one bit. It was something I tried out – I came, I saw, I decided, no."

"But in this case, you owe a reason," Faysal said. "This is not like you went to the bakery, and the bread being old and hard, you didn't buy."

"I don't know. There could be many reasons."

"One of which might be that you are careless?" Suham said.

All the men and Saleema turned towards her.

"You want everyone to accommodate you." Her expression was so smooth, that the words didn't seem to be slipping out of her lips.

Michael bent his head.

"Rita told me a secret once that I took as a joke," she said. "That the first time the two of you broke up, you'd mentioned to her that you might, when in America, change your mind and come back to marry her."

"I didn't ask her to wait for me, though."

"No, you didn't. But you gave her hope. What is the difference?"

He bent his head again.

"You know how to yell at us, and you know how to spoil yourself amongst us, and you know how to blame us," she said, mechanically. "But that's all you know, Michael. That's all."

The telephone then rang. It was the man from the bakery, asking what time was best to deliver the wedding cake. "Anytime," she said, since it had been already paid for.

When she hung up the phone, whoever had been looking at her moved their eyes away, in case she'd turn on them as well. "Would you be so kind as to take a walk outside with me?" she asked Saad, needing a great deal of fresh air, as well as a companion whom she'd be able to handle rudely, without him getting his feelings hurt.

Saad was so surprised he couldn't answer right away, so Faysal did it for him. "That's a terrific idea. You two do that while we sit with Michael a little longer."

Saad and Suham left the apartment.   As she walked, she felt as weak as when she'd given birth, but without the physical pain.   She watched the people around her; the veiled woman with the child, the student with books, the loitering men with cigarettes, the bartender blending strawberries, bananas and oranges.   She wished she could trade places with any one of them, just so she wouldn't face Wadi's disappointment, Rita's sadness, and Michael's meanness.

Saad bought her ice cream, even though she had insisted he shouldn't.

"It'll help you forget," he said, handing the cone to her.   She looked at him like he knew what he was talking about.   She wasn't in the mood to correct anyone.

She made him walk for miles, because she didn't expect to go home to a transformed Michael.   She wished there was an airplane at the bus stop that could fly her home, so she could drink Turkish coffee and smoke a cigarette while staring out the window until George came from work, kissed her forehead, and soothed her spirits.

"By the way," Saad blurted, disconnecting her thoughts from the window that faced Charleston Street.   "Michael gave me a thousand dollars to hand over to Rita personally."

Her footsteps ceased at once, and frowning, she lifted her eyes to Saad's.   He must have grasped her confusion, because he explained the matter.   "It's to compensate for her and her mother's travel fees, and some other expenses."

Suham looked at the ground in silence, and then she laughed bitterly. The transfer of money from Michael's pocket to Saad's happened right in front of her, without her realizing it. And poor Faysal and his friends were under the impression that, if they hung around the apartment long enough, they'd alter Michael's decision.

"I'd hate to ask anything of you under such dreadful circumstances," he said. "But can you, please, accompany me? I feel it inappropriate to go there alone."

"Of course, you cannot go there alone!" Suham said. "This gesture would only wound Rita's heart more. Besides, I'd like to see her. I want to be sure she's feeling well."

Chapter 25

❧

uham and Saad put their heads together to remember Rita's new address. A taxi drove them to the house, and when they arrived Suham looked at Saad and took a deep breath. Then she knocked on the door.

"*Ahlan wa'sahlen*," Najat greeted them. Then she invited them in, and when they took their seats on the family room couch, she asked whether they preferred tea or coffee.

"Please, don't trouble yourself," Suham said.

"You must drink something," Najat insisted.

Saad intervened here, before the women went back and forth ten additional times, each one mirroring the other's politeness. "Coffee sounds good," he said.

"Can I see Rita?" Suham asked, before Najat disappeared into the kitchen.

"*Itfathali*," Najat welcomed. "She's in the bedroom, if you'll just follow me."

Rita was lying on the bed. Her beauty had survived, despite the misfortune that had fallen upon her, but her glow was gone. Najat complained to Rita about the servant not yet having returned with the lamb shanks, which she needed in order to cook the bulgur. Suham was curious to inquire more about this servant, but under the circumstances, she did not dare.

Najat then excused herself and walked out.

As Suham sat down on a chair in the corner of the room, Rita got off the bed and began undressing in front of the mirror. "What is he doing now?" she asked, without turning to Suham.

"Sitting amongst six or seven men – and Saleema."

"Hmm, Saleema is there too!" Rita sneered, but then she controlled her agony by pursing her lips tight and keeping her eyes straightforward. "And what has he to say to them?"

"That he does not want to get married."

She paused, and a thought made her wince. She pulled on her jeans and zipped them with a harsh motion. Then she slipped a black blouse over her brassiere and fastened the buttons with nervous fingers. "And what did they have to say?"

"That he cannot be so insensible as to pass up a lady like you."

She looked hard at the mirror. "That man Faysal," she jeered. "In Baghdad, he couldn't get within four feet of me, much less talk to me. Then Michael comes along, and he plays me like a toy in front of all of them."

A few tears trickled down Rita's pale cheeks, causing Suham's eyes to moisten. "Had I known –"

Rita wiped away her tears and finally looked at Suham. "You're not to blame. He's not a child."

To not be blamed was no comfort for Suham. A happiness was snatched from everyone's hand, and as though it was a baby, Suham knew the damaging results would take years to erase.

Saad knocked on the door, and after being invited

in, he asked to have a word alone with Rita. They stepped out of the room for a few minutes, and when they returned, Saad and Suham prepared to leave.

"We won't say our goodbyes yet," Suham said, standing on the front porch with Rita and her mother.

"I didn't assume we would." Rita then smiled. "It would upset me if we'd conclude this expedition today of all days."

"Did you give her the money?" Suham asked Saad in the taxi ride back to their apartment.

"Yes."

"And what did she say?"

"Nothing."

"Nothing?" Suham was surprised. Even though the American dollar was incredibly strong in Iraq's exchange market, considering Rita's wealth, a thousand dollars was mere pocket change. She should have refused it. "Did she just take it?"

"She just took it."

"Oh." Rita must have been more resentful than she'd shown, Suham thought. The poor girl didn't realize that spending Michael's money would burn her, rather than console her.

The apartment was dark and smelled of a dozen odors; cigarette smoke, coffee beans, the perfume and food spices Saleema had imported from her oven and her dresser, the colognes and perspiration the men had carried over from their medicine cabinets and the busy streets.

While Michael lay on the couch, staring glumly at the ceiling, and Rita perched on her bed, crying into her pillow, the spectators of this morning's affair were either debating the issue, analyzing it or simply musing over it.

"Did you want me to stay?" Saad asked, looking over at the couch where Michael laid.

"No, but thank you," she said. "You've been terrific, really."

He slightly bowed his head and took his leave.

"Did you eat?" she heard Michael say.

"No, did you?"

"No." He kept quiet for a few seconds. "Do you want to walk to a booth and get sandwiches?"

"Yes." She wanted to get out of this apartment. It was smeared with so much ugliness, she wished she could cut it with a scissors and toss it in the garbage, like she'd once done with a dress of Nisreen's after a stray dog had vomited on it.

As though one was a rock and the other a leaf, they did not exchange a word. Contrary to her expectations, this walk made Suham feel ill. It prompted her to replay the work she'd put into this wedding, starting in America first; from visiting strange girls' homes, to calling George's cousin Fatin, to the florist, the reception hall, the dinner gatherings held in Michael's honor, the *asrunia* to bid Suham goodbye. And finishing off with Jordan; from being ecstatic the day Michael met Rita and he decided to marry her, to the doubts he had, then the certainty, then the crash.

"Michael," she said quietly, as though not to disturb the bustling streets. "Do you have someone in America?"

"I don't know."

Suham had never been slapped by a man, but she knew it must feel something like this; a painful blow that made the body tremble, not harming the face, only the heart. "You've deceived us then," she said, and with tears touching her lips, she walked away.

In the dark, on the road, she sobbed as she hadn't

done for years, until all her strength and all her power were wrung so tight, she felt numb. And in that state she appeared at Rita's door.

Rita's eyes enlarged with concern upon seeing Suham. "*Ya rabbi*," she prayed. "I hope everything is alright!"

Suham brought herself to smile. "Don't get too excited, *habbibti*. Saleema took me to her place, while Michael went out with Saad. They haven't come back, though. I don't think they know that I don't have a key."

"Well, then, you must spend the night here," Najat said. "You don't know what time he's coming home, and at this hour, you can't be going back and forth alone in a taxi."

"But Michael might get worried if he doesn't find me," Suham continued to lie, to divert the truth as far away from their minds as possible. Their perception of Michael was already bad enough.

"He'd assume you either spent the night at Saleema's or you came here," Rita said. "We have a phone, but it only receives calls." She then laughed. "And we don't even know its number."

They asked if she was hungry.

"A little."

Najat then recited the foods in her refrigerator; burgul, yogurt, cheese, olives and eggplant puree.

"Cheese and bread will do," Suham said.

They kept her company while she ate, and then they all went to bed, Najat in one room, Rita and Suham in the other. Rita handed Suham a royal blue silk nightgown, revealing like hers, placed a pillow on Suham's side of the bed, fluffed it, and asked if she needed anything else.

"No, thank you." Suham hadn't been pampered since she'd last seen her husband, and she desperately missed it. That night, with the soft pillow beneath her head, the cool silk nightgown against her legs, and the perfumed bed sheet around her shoulders, she realized that the way George served her did not show weakness, but strength. Had it been an easy job, God would have sent her a different husband, someone more like Michael.

The next morning Suham and Rita sat in the window-covered patio and awaited the breakfast Najat was preparing in the kitchen. Like an umbrella, many trees hung over the patio, so the ladies had the freedom to remain in their nightgowns without wearing robes.

"Where is your servant?" Suham remembered to ask.

Rita laughed as she pointed her finger to the left. "There."

Suham was unable to see where she meant, and Rita laughed even more. "There!"

Suham then noticed a wooden door, and she frowned. It looked like a huge cooking pot, the kind used for making famous foods, like *harissa*, *pacha*, or *tashreeb*, was tucked inside the wall, with only its lid showing.

Rita raised her brows and nodded. "Yes, there! He scared me the other day, when I called out his name, Abu-Ahmad, Abu-Ahmad and his head popped out of that hole, like a dog's."

Suham joined Rita's laughter.

"He is included with the rent. I was surprised that the apartment complexes didn't have a regular servant."

Najat came out with a tray of tea, set it on the table and returned to the kitchen. Rita told Suham how dirty their place had been when they'd moved into it. "It was greasy and it had cockroaches," she said. "Saudi Arabian students lived here before us. They're so rich and spoiled."

Something up ahead caught Rita's eye and she crossed her legs and smiled. "You see that house with the rug hanging from the balcony?"

Suham looked in that direction.

"There's a young girl that lives there, about fifteen or sixteen years old, and she is so bad. Whenever she comes out, she teases the boy who lives above us."

Suham arched her brows and grinned. "Really?"

Rita's smile widened as she swung her leg up and down. "The other day, she came out wearing a black shirt that came down to here." She placed her finger between her breasts, slightly above her stomach. "Down to here," she emphasized, pressing her finger harder against her bones. "She drove the poor boy crazy."

"*Inshallah* he didn't have an exam that day," Suham prayed and they giggled.

Najat brought out a plate of cheese, tomatoes and green olives, with a bag of bread. In the middle of breakfast, she left to make a pot of Turkish coffee. Suham took this opportunity to ask Rita what she planned on doing now.

"My mother and I might stay in Jordan for three or four months, depending on circumstances," she said. "That's why we had rented this place."

Suham didn't question what those circumstances might be, but assumed it meant another suitor. She hoped so, since Rita getting married would greatly ease her conscience. Suham then asked what had happened in the bedroom the night before the wedding.

With a sad smile, Rita thought momentarily. "Michael was staring at me, and I asked him why, but he

wouldn't answer. So I got off the bed and told him I
didn't like being compared to anyone."

Suham sighed, heavily.

"He didn't defend himself, he only suggested that
I come to America through a fiancée visa. He said he
couldn't guarantee we'd marry, but he promised me a
furnished apartment and a job." She laughed, shaking her head. "Don't worry about me. I'll manage. I
will."

After breakfast, Rita and her mother asked Suham to stay for lunch. She thanked them for their
hospitality, but said it was necessary for her to return
home. "I don't want to worry Michael," she said. "And
I have to pack."

Rita nodded her head in understanding.

"I will see you before I leave."

"You must."

When she arrived at the apartment, she and Michael went to Royal Jordanian's airline headquarters,
and asked to change their departure dates.

"To which day, sir?" the man behind the counter
asked.

"Tomorrow."

The man typed things in the computer and observed the screen, as closely as Suham's travel agent
had done. "I have two seats available for tomorrow's
flight."

"Cool!"

When Saad heard the news, he rushed over to
their place. They ate dinner and drank tea in silence.
To break the tension, Saad told a story of a lady who'd
done her hair at the salon, appeared at the church
and waited to witness the ceremony, attend the party
and eat lots of food. When the priest informed her
that the wedding was cancelled, she was shocked.

"She's probably home cursing you, Michael," Saad said. "If she knew where you lived, she'd make you reimburse her."

No one slept that night because their hectic schedule did not permit it; they had to pack their luggage, make a stop at Rita's house very early in the morning, so Suham could say goodbye, and make it to the airport on time.

The next morning, they secured the luggage in the truck of the taxi and they gave the driver Rita's address. "Stop there first," Suham told him.

Michael asked the driver to park some twenty feet away from the house. "Give her my regards," he said to his aunt, his voice choking.

Suham tightened her jaw to stop from crying and got out of the car. When she rang the door, Rita came out in the royal blue robe she'd worn inside their first apartment, when their problems were just starting.

"We are leaving for the airport."

Rita drew her robe tighter around her body and glanced to the left. "Where's Michael?"

"He's in the car."

"I want to see him before he goes."

They walked towards the cab. Michael must have noticed Rita coming because he stepped out of the car, wearing a warm smile.

She approached him slowly. "So you are leaving?"

"Yes."

"I wish you the best of luck."

"And I, the same."

She looked to the ground and then back to him, with a splendid smile this time, to assure him there were no hard feelings. As both their eyes moistened with tears, Rita returned to Suham and took her hands. "Send me the pictures we took together.

Please don't forget."

Suham looked at the soft creature who stood in front of her and she desired, more than anything else, to change her fate. If she could only bring Rita into the car with them, as was originally planned, and have her cross the ocean and land in a foreign land, wearing her blue robe and pink slippers.

"I want to see you again," Suham said, her tears beginning to boil over her eyelids and onto her lashes.

Rita looked down. "I don't know if I'm going back to Baghdad."

Suham smiled at her. "Is he in America?"

"Belgium."

Suham's eyes gave her the most tender stare.

Rita turned to Michael, and then to Suham again. "Whatever happened between me and Michael does not change what happened between us."

Suham blinked in a long and slow motion, and her tears gradually fell. The ladies then smiled at each other, kissed and hugged goodbye, and Suham got inside the car. As the car reversed itself to the end of the street, Rita waved to them. In her royal blue robe, in the midst of the half-light, half-dark street, she looked like a dream that was going to the hands of God as one awoke from it.

Chapter 26

hey went into a restaurant in Kennedy airport because Suham wanted a sandwich. Michael was hungry too but said he'd wait in case TWA served them a meal. Suham stared at the menu on the wall and decided on a wild mushroom and rice sandwich wrap.

Michael winced. "That sounds sick!"

He then gave the lady at the register a hundred dollar bill and apologized that he didn't have anything smaller. "See, we just came from the Moon docks."

The lady smiled, while Suham looked at him disapprovingly.

"What?" he cried.

"You shouldn't be acting so carefree."

"You know, that's the exact same thing you told me at my father's funeral."

He startled her, and she looked at him with sympathy. His humor shouldn't mislead her; he was in no less pain than she. They sat in a booth, across from each other, in silence. She ate her sandwich cautiously, with tiny bites and in slow motion, as though it was made of live serpent and not wild mushrooms. Michael looked off to the left. "I guess a lot of Jews live here, don't they?" he said.

Suham looked at the men in black hats and black coats with curls hanging from the side of their ears, like exquisite jewelry. "They seem so refined."

"Yeah, they're pretty cool."

They were silent again. Suham imagined the Jews' wives and daughters, their mothers and sisters, at their old fashioned homes, baking delicious breads, while dressed in graceful traditional gowns that flared against their ankles like wind when they walked and puffed around their waists like a cake when they sat.

Then in a sudden jerk, Michael turned towards Suham. "Do you hate me?"

Taken aback, Suham paused a little, letting the wild mushroom and rice sit in her mouth as a few tears stung her eyes. "A little."

He patted the stack of napkins set over her tray, flipped them over, and patted them again. He repeated this process four times. "Well, that's alright."

She looked at him hard. "You don't understand, Michael. I went through more work in that one month than I did in a lifetime."

"Well, me too!" he huffed. "But you don't see me hating you – a little."

Her eyes on the table, she paused, smiled and shook her head. "This may take a while."

"What, for you to be nice to me again?"

"No, for your conscience to start working."

"So what?" he grumbled. "Your conscience never worked, but you don't see me complaining."

"Michael!"

"Everyone hates how you treat George."

Frowning, she leaned her chest over the table. "But he doesn't and neither do you."

"That's only because you manipulate us with your okra and your *kubba*."

She sat back and thought a moment. "I don't

think George was half as bothered about how I treated him, as much as he was about me not being happy."

"Same thing," he mumbled.

She squinted and looked at him harder. "Who is she, Michael?"

"Who is who?" he asked, bewildered.

"The girl you compared Rita to."

His eyes jumped over the table, like a Spanish dancer with fifty layered green, purple and yellow ruffles radiantly swaying in the air, the way the flags of all the nations would look if washed and hung out to air-dry on a windy but sunny afternoon. "I don't know."

"Is she American?"

"Okay, get this!" he said, excited. "I asked Rita once if she would've married me had I not come from America, had I been some ordinary guy living in Iraq, and you know what she said?"

Suham waited patiently.

"That she didn't know." His lips pressed each word as though he was squeezing an orange for juice.

She arched her brows. "And you did not admire her for her honesty?"

He looked confused for a second, tried to defend himself, but stopped and started to look around again.

"Are you going to marry that whoever?" she asked.

"No!"

"Does she even exist?"

"I don't know, really."

She shook her head, then sighed. "I used to walk on this floor –" She glanced at the restaurant's gray tile. "But my head was –" Her eyes loped high as she raised her arm above her head and swung it behind her shoulders. "I thought by doing this, I'd secure my sixteen years of living in Baghdad, and in return, preserve my identity."

She paused and laughed with sarcasm. "But in Jordan I wondered, what about this identity?" She pointed to the gold cross that centered directly between her breasts and just above her cleavage. "I'd held on so dearly to the past, that I nearly lost this."

"Then you shouldn't be hating me – a little," he stressed. "You should be thanking me, damn it."

She grinned. "You're not going to let me win, are you?"

"If you want, I will."

"No, I don't want," she said, quickly, then pondered for a moment. "We should've given Saad some money. For all the trouble, and because he needs it..."

"I did. Three hundred dollars."

Suham was surprised, and touched.

His hand over his stomach, Michael started laughing, and she asked him what was funny. "Aunt Sabria will be real pissed about the peanut butter cans. Real pissed."

Suham smiled, because she knew it was true. Then she sighed. She was anxious to return to her kitchen and make her nephew his favorite recipes and flatter herself watching him eat with a hearty appetite and have fun helping Wadi tame her only son. She was anxious to guard playfully against Lisa's high spirits and to be in George's arms, the way a baby kangaroo was to be in its mother's pouch.

The curtains were drawn, and from her bed, Suham could see Lisa's summer dress flutter as she went out to get the newspaper, with a cup of coffee in her hand, and a head band, the color of Rita's royal blue robe, over her blonde hair. Suham never read newspapers, because they would stain her fingers. Besides, the papers were just like TV news broadcasters; they gave her misleading concepts about America, a country that had a lot more mystery than it did crime.

Suham turned towards George, who was still asleep, and she observed every feature; the brows that frowned at her when she teased, the jaw that tightened when she misbehaved, the lips that kissed her when she conducted herself well, and the eyes that always, always adored her.

She kissed his eyelids, and as though it was a reflex test at the doctor's office, he instantly opened them. He looked at her in a daze, and she smiled, mischievously. "Do you know who I am?"

"Of course, I know who you are," he mumbled, half asleep.

Her smile widened. "Do you know what my name means?"

"Hmm?" And he tucked his head into the pillow.

She stroked her finger over his shoulder while observing her placid self in the mirror. "What is my name, George?"

"Hmm," he moaned. "Suham."

"What does it mean?"

He partially lifted his head towards her and looked confused. "In literature?"

"Yes. Tell me."

He focused hard, then cleared his throat. "It's *suhum* – masculine, plural, *suham* if singular – in the Arabic scripture." He took a deep breath and continued more lazily. "And, it means arrows."

She smiled and lay on her back. "Does it suit me?"

"Hum, hum."

"How?"

"I don't know, Suham, *habbibti*," he groaned. "I'm not good at that kind of stuff."

She stared at the ceiling. "I am not the same arrow I used to be, you know," she said, but wasn't sure he heard. "I am different. I don't shoot my roots outside anymore."

He opened his eyes wide and looked at her. She smiled, because he'd heard.

"Don't you see I am different?"

"Yes."

"Do you still love me?"

"Yes."

She kissed his forehead with the softness of her lips and the moisture of a single tear. "I don't want to be so much in control anymore," she whispered. "Not anymore."

"Okay."

Her mother once told her that every pot had its lid, an old Iraqi saying that meant each person had a soul mate. And that when the pot and its lid were sealed together, and the flavor of the spices and the heat of the fire worked privately inside, the taste of the food was much enhanced before it was served to guests. "You be like this with your husband," she'd told Suham, making a fist with her hand. "And you will better serve God."

THE END